18 Tales of Romance, Adventure, Suspense and Humor

Kiran Kumar Singh

Ukiyoto Publishing

All global publishing rights are held by

Ukiyoto Publishing

Published in 2024

ISBN 9789367958728

www.ukiyoto.com

Dedication

This book is dedicated to the memory of my father Dr. R. K. Singh, mother Mrs. Suraj Kumari Singh and my wife Mrs. Reba Rautela Singh. The former was a noted educationist. In my childhood he encouraged me to read and write outside the school curriculum. My mother retired as the Professor and Head of the Education Department of the RBS College at Agra and helped me in English Grammar at the school level. My wife was a qualified and talented artist. She encouraged me to write. May their souls rest in peace.

Preface and Acknowledgement

The book includes eighteen fictional stories which are meant for all age groups above twelve. These cover a range of romance, adventure, humor, and suspense. Stories numbered 1, 6, and 10 are primarily romantic tales while no. 15 is a comic romance. Stories 2 and 13 are adventure stories dealing with hunting. Number 3 is an adventure story dealing with crime and suspense. Stories 4, 7, 8, 12, 16 and 18 deal with humor and contain anecdotes of school and college life. Story 5 can be classified as a science fiction adventure with a commentary on the direction taken by science and technology and its dangerous consequences. I would define story 9 as a philosophical adventure and story 11 as a satirical adventure. Story 17 is an adventure story about ghosts. The reason why most stories have an element of humor is because I feel people need to smile and laugh more. The readers are free to categorize the stories according to their opinions. Feedback of their views is most welcome and will be useful.

I gratefully acknowledge the efforts of my sister Ms Preeti Singh, a highly qualified teacher of English Literature, my son Gaurav and my friend Ms. Savita Singh, a noted author, for their help and advice.

****

Contents

The Punjabi Boy's Dreams

Rohan was born in Amritsar in 1942, when the British still ruled India. He was a bright and thoughtful boy. His father was a prosperous shopkeeper and could afford to educate him at one of the English medium schools. One of his teachers used to say, "Children if you want to achieve something in life then you must have big dreams, but you must work hard to make your dreams come true. He also told them, "When you are nervous and cannot think clearly you must breathe deeply and remember god." These were the most sensible lessons he learned at school.

He did not want to become a shopkeeper. His elder brother could inherit the shop. He dreamed of studying as much as possible and settling down in America as a professor in a good university. He had a good friend, Vikram whose older cousin was studying for MS in Engineering in America, after getting a BTech degree from an IIT. He visited Vikram during summer vacations and Rohan met him. From him he learnt that the best way to go to America is to do Bachelor of Engineering in India and then get good scores in the GRE and TOEFL and get admission for MS along with a research or teaching assistantship.

From then onwards he dreamed of studying engineering in India and then going to America. He put in every effort to make his dreams come true. While attempting the IIT, GRE and TOEFL tests he would breathe deeply and remember god and succeeded in getting into an IIT with a scholarship. Later he got a research assistantship and admission for MS Electrical Engineering at Ohio University, Athens, USA in the early sixties.

The first few days at Ohio were hectic. He found suitable accommodation and had a couple of meetings with his Professor to choose the subjects and schedule the research work. Classes were from eight to eleven and work from one to five, with a two hour lunch break. The next week there was a welcome function for the new students where he joined the queue of students waiting to be greeted by the varsity president who shook the hand of each newcomer who stood in the line. He joined the line behind a tall, slim and beautiful girl. She turned around, smiled and said, "Hi, I am Susan Ricci, but you may call me Suzy."

Rohan felt that she was the prettiest girl he had seen. She was even prettier than Gina Lollobrigida whom he had seen in the movie Come September. He replied, "I am Rohan from India."

"Have you seen the Taj Mahal," she asked.

"No," he said and seeing her look of surprise he added, "Maybe someday we may see it together."

She laughed and he added, "I am starting my MS in Electrical Engineering."

"You are way ahead," she replied, "I am just starting my BA. But my brother Antony is two years ahead of me."

Now it was her turn to be greeted by the President and then Rohan's. The President held his hand and asked him where he was from and whether he had adjusted well. Rohan wanted to follow Susan but the President kept talking with him for a few minutes. By this time she had joined a group of boys and girls all chatting away. Rohan felt too shy to barge in and join her so he walked over to the refreshment table and took a cold drink and started chatting with a PhD student. He kept looking at Susan hoping that she would come out of the group but she soon left with the group.

The next few weeks he was very busy, but he still thought of Susan. Besides a pretty face, she had the friendliest smile he had ever seen. One day while going for lunch he changed his route and passed behind the library instead of the front. He saw Susan coming from the opposite direction. While crossing she smiled and said, "Hi, Rohan."

"Hi, Suzy" he responded and she was far away before he could react further. From then onwards he always took the path behind the library and they crossed each other and the same greetings were exchanged. Each time he wanted to stop her and talk but his nerve would fail him at the last moment. On the seventh crossing he blocked her path and said, "Wait a minute, I have something important to talk to you about."

She replied, "Sorry, I have to rush for lunch, then rest a bit and go for afternoon classes."

"Is it ok if I walk with you and talk at the same time?"

"Ok" she responded.

"You are the prettiest girl I have seen in my life," he blurted out, "and I would like to marry you as soon as I get my degree and get a good job."

She laughed and said, "I only know you as Rohan from India, and we talked for a few minutes. In America we think about marriage after dating and getting to know each other well, but you are proposing to me so suddenly."

"Please let me be your friend and meet you once in a while," he requested.

"That sounds better, but no serious dating. My father is paying for my education and expects me to get only A's and B's in all courses. He is a school drop-out and has worked hard to start a construction company. He has warned me against dating and marriage until I get my degree. The same rule applies to my brother Antony who will join his company only after he earns a BA degree."

"He seems to be a very strict father," was Rohan's response.

By this time they had reached the girls sorority where she stayed. She gave him the phone number and told him that on most weekends she visited her parents at Logan a town about fifty miles away. After this they met a couple of times a week in the student's cafeteria and drank tea or coffee and talked a lot about their likes and dislikes, their past lives and their families. Sometimes they went to the pizzeria for a pizza or watched a movie. She insisted on sharing of all expenses. He felt very happy in her company, but she insisted that they were just friends and nothing more. He proposed marriage several times.

Each time she replied, "I will get married only after BA and with my father's approval. I respect him and he loves and cares for me and wants what is best for me. One day I will ask my mother to invite you to our house so you can talk with him. He is a tyrant, but deep down inside he has a heart of gold."

A few days after this, she asked him to visit their house at Logan and talk with her father, only if he was in a good mood. Rohan had reached their house before ten in the morning on a Saturday, so that he could talk with her father before her other friends arrived. It was Mrs. Ricci's idea to invite him along with some of Susan's friends as inviting Rohan alone might upset Mr. Ricci.

That morning Rohan had travelled from Athens, Ohio and reached their house in Logan early and rung the bell. It was Susan who opened the door and said, "Bad news, dad got a call from his foreman about some problems at the construction site. He is in a terrible mood and is studying the construction drawings in his office down in the basement. He will leave for the site as soon as his partner Mr. Johnson reaches here. Before he got the call he was in a good mood and was looking forward to meet my college friends, but now I don't think you will get a chance to talk with him about us."

She introduced him to her brother, Antony and mother, Sophia. They sat and talked for a while. It was mainly Mrs. Ricci who asked him a lot of questions about himself and his family. This stopped as soon as Susan's other friends arrived. Then Mrs. Ricci kept going to the kitchen frequently to attend to the lunch.

After some time Mr. Ricci strode into the drawing room looking rather grim. He was a tall broad shouldered, tough looking man. Rohan wondered how he could be the father of a girl as beautiful as Susan. Ignoring the guests, Mr. Ricci addressed his wife, "Sophia, that confounded Johnson has not shown up yet. I will wait outside in the car studying these drawing and leave exactly at ten forty whether he is here or not. If he shows up later tell him to reach the site pronto."

After this he had walked out of the front door and Rohan had followed him out after a pause. Now it was ten thirty and he had less than ten minutes to talk with him. He had walked to his car with an air of nonchalance, but inside he felt like an unarmed man walking into a lion's den. He stood near the driver's window and Mr. Ricci glared at him as he spoke in his politest manner, "Sir, I want to talk with you about an important matter. As you are a busy man I will come straight to the point. It concerns Susan and me. We both like each other and she has asked me to request you to approve our friendship."

Mr. Ricci's face reddened and he looked at Rohan as a hungry lion looks at its prey just before pouncing on it. Then his expression softened and he said, "You must be Suzy's friend about whom Sophia mentioned last night, but she didn't say that you were coming today with her other friends. She also didn't say anything about you being a foreigner. Well if Suzy likes you, I must talk with you. I am in a hurry so hop into the car."

As he drove he said, "My father and mother were born in Italy and married there. They migrated to America when I was little. I married an Italian girl in America, but what does my daughter do? She makes friends with a kid who is not even an American. You are probably not Catholic and most likely not even a Christian. What the hell! I suppose if a man wants his daughter to study in college he must let her choose her friends. Now tell me everything about yourself."

Rohan replied, "I am Rohan from India, by religion a Hindu, but I respect all religions equally. I am studying for an MS in Electrical Engineering at Ohio U. I work in my department as a research assistant to finance my studies. It is not really a job but a kind of scholarship."

Mr. Ricci responded, "It is nice to meet a kid who earns for his education. My parents came to America when I was two. Life was tough for them. Both of them worked, but my father died while I was still in school. All of my brothers and sisters had to drop out of school and go to work to keep the family afloat. Today I am rich, but I had to struggle hard to get what I have. I want both of my kids to complete their college degrees with good grades. That is very important for me, because I am a school dropout."

Then he drove in silence till they reached the construction site. Before getting out of the car he said, "It will take me all day to sort out the problems here, but we can talk in between and also when we have lunch. There's a nice Italian restaurant nearby where we can eat so you better hang around. Maybe you will learn something about construction.

Everything turned out nicely. They ate spaghetti and meatballs with tasty bread, butter and cheese and a delicious salad, followed by ice cream with chocolate sauce. Mr. Ricci did most of the talking.

He said, "You asked for my permission to be friends with Susan. That reminds me of Italian traditions. Before my father married my mother in Italy, he took her father's permission to be her suitor and they were married when she approved. I was in America so I did no such thing. When I was interested in Sophia, her father warned me to stay away from her otherwise he would punch my nose. He did not want his daughter to marry a high school dropout. That didn't stop us and finally he agreed to our marriage."

After a pause he continued, "Things are different now my boy, but remember, right now I am only approving your friendship. For marriage ask my permission after she gets her degree, if you both are still interested. Another thing, she is a catholic and after marriage her husband has to take her to a catholic church at least once a month."

Then he asked Rohan if he liked the meal. When he answered in the affirmative, he said "What we ate here is half Italian and half American. Sophia is the best Italian cook in America. You would have got much better food at home."

Rohan replied, "I hope I get a chance to eat one of her meals."

"You certainly will." he replied.

Then they spent some more time at the site and drove back home. By then the other boys and girls had left. The happy expression on Rohan's face told Susan, Sophia and Antony that everything had worked out well. Mr. Ricci said, "Now we all will have coffee and watch the football match on TV."

They watched the match and chatted for a while, but nothing was said about Susan and Rohan. Then Rohan said, "It's time for me to catch the bus back to Athens, and thank you all for making my visit so pleasant."

Mr. Ricci asked Antony and Susan to drive Rohan to the bus stand. On the way Rohan said, "Your father certainly has a heart of gold. Today I feel even happier than I had felt on getting admission at Ohio."

After her father's approval of their friendship, she was much more relaxed in his company. He soon convinced her that they should get married after he completed his MS. Then he would study for a PhD and she could complete BA. It took a lot more effort to get Mr. Ricci's approval, which he gave only on condition that he would pay all of Suzy's study expenses till she completed her BA.

They had a wonderful church wedding in Logan, followed by an Indian wedding in Amritsar, also attended by her parents and brother. Two years later he was awarded his PhD and she her BA degree at the same convocation. After that he was appointed as a faculty member at Ohio and she took a job. Soon children came along- two boys with a girl in between.

They had a very happy life and would go on long visits to India. His career blossomed and he was appointed at the prestigious, Harvard University as a Professor. The children finished their studies, got jobs, married and settled down and they became grandparents. Soon they were celebrating their fiftieth wedding anniversary with their children, grandchildren, Antony's family and relations from India.

Late in the evening the grandchildren surprised them by conducting a mock wedding ceremony. The children chanted, "Now you may kiss the bride."

Susan, who had aged gracefully, looked even prettier than ever, and they kissed. Everyone applauded and the doorbell started ringing and continued even after they stopped kissing. No one else seemed to have heard the bell. Rohan entered the lobby to open the front door.

Suddenly the scene changed and he realized that he was lying in bed with an alarm clock ringing on the bedside table. He switched it off and saw that the room was the one in which he had stayed as a student when he had come to Ohio. Was it an old memory or a hallucination? It seemed very real. He wondered whether their marriage, children and everything else was simply a dream. It seemed so real and vivid that it could not have been just a dream. His mind was confused. He took a deep breath and prayed to god. Soon his mind became clear.

He realized that the alarm had rung to wake him up for the morning classes. He remembered that he had met Susan and they had crossed each other behind the library six times, but there had been no seventh crossing, no visit to Logan, no meeting with Mr. Ricci, no courtship or marriage, no children or grand children and no fiftieth anniversary. It had all been a dream- the most wonderful dream that he had ever had.

He had crossed paths six times with the most beautiful girl in the world. Each time she had responded with a big smile. Why had he not stopped her and asked her for a date- because he was being stupid and cowardly. He gave himself a hard slap on the face and said, "Rohan, what kind of a Punjabi boy are you? You are so timid that God has had to wake you up, so don't let him down."

He got ready quickly and rushed off to class. That day, on his way back, he was determined to talk with her and make this dream come true like his other dreams. After all he had received divine guidance.

****

The Guardian of the Forest

A man-eating tiger had made its presence felt in the hills of Himachal and Uttara Khand. It had been steadily increasing its human kills, averaging two a month for the last eight months. It did most of its hunting on the outskirts of villages or on the lesser travelled mountain paths. The tiger would lie in wait for its prey, concealed in bushes and pounce when it came close. In this way many cattle, goats or humans were killed and dragged away into the forest.

Those who saw the tiger were all agreed on three things. It had a collar on its neck, it could not run fast because of a limp and though large in size it was skinny. Several times after a human kill search parties went after it with shot guns or rifles, but could not kill it. Either they could not find it, or if they did, it would slink away before anyone could get a shot.

Tigers mostly hunt their prey at night and sleep during the day, but this one hunted mostly during the day. Their normal prey is wild game and they generally keep away from human settlements. This one had become a man eater because of its inability to run fast. It had sustained some injury while chasing prey or in a fight with another tiger or maybe a gunshot wound. Thus it could not chase and catch wild prey in the forests. It had to rely on stealth and cunning to catch prey near the villages and on forest paths.

The fact that it was skinny meant that it did not get enough to eat. This was because quite often it could not eat its kill. The large and noisy search parties would disturb it before it could eat enough. Hunger forced it to hunt even during daytime. Its collar confirmed that it had been shot with a dart to tranquilize it and a radio collar put on it to track its movements.

At first its kills were reported in the local papers on the inner pages. When its menace grew, reports started appearing as front page headlines. Soon it became the hottest news item. The national dailies, the TV channels and radio news all gave it the topmost billing. It was compared with the famous man eaters of a century ago- the most notorious being the Champawat man eater which had killed more than four hundred people and was shot by Jim Corbett.

Compared to four hundred its score of sixteen was a modest figure. Still one cannot be insensitive to the killing of fellow humans. Even one person killed creates much sorrow and anger in the hearts of the near and dear ones.

Soon questions were raised in the assemblies of the two states in which it had made its kills. The issue was even raised in the parliament. By now the public was also in a state of frenzy. In their imagination the tiger had become a bigger menace than the Pakistani terrorists. Such was the terror created by it, that the two affected states saw a fall in the number of tourists.

At first the menace was being tackled at the level of the district, where the District Magistrate would summon all of the Tehsildars and ask them to ensure the safety of people and live stock in their areas and give relief to victims. The Tehsildars would visit the villages and meet the headmen and others to caution them about the menace and to issue alerts in case of sighting the tiger. Later the Commissioners took the threat seriously. They would summon all of the District Magistrates under them and ensure that the tiger alert was coordinated in all of the districts. No doubt their combined efforts resulted in the saving of the lives of many humans and live stock.

As soon as the tiger was sighted, an alarm would be raised. Men would come out with lathis, axes, spears, firearms, drums and bugles. The procession would proceed towards the place of the tiger sighting, beating drums and bugles. The awful din would drive the man-eater away.

It had been chased and driven away many times. It developed a counter strategy of its own. Whenever it made a kill, it would drag the carcass for many miles into deep forest and eat its meal in peace. Then it would get its much needed rest and sleep. After that it would make its way out of that area and look for a new hunting ground. Despite being lame, it managed to cover vast distances over many districts in the states of Himachal Pradesh and Uttara Khand. Some news reports even stated that more than one tiger was involved.

When questions were raised in the state assemblies and the parliament, the chief ministers of the two states ordered a coordinated hunt. Three dozen marksmen were selected for this. Some were expert hunters; others were army men who had hunted Pakistani terrorists in the forest areas of Jammu and Kashmir. They were given a crash course on how to hunt a man eating tiger and discussions were held to decide on the best strategy. Some suggested that it be tranquilized with a dart and then put in some zoo. This was over ruled, giving the argument that a man eater would be a menace to the zoo staff. Someone suggested that the tiger should be tracked using its radio collar and shot. The limitations were that the signal had a range of only two or three kilometers. The collar had become old and defective and the signal had become intermittent.

Finally a plan was adopted. It was decided to divide the group into teams of six hunters in each team. They were allotted their own regions. Villagers were instructed to report its sighting and not to disturb it. They were advised to stay in their homes with all of their cattle. After the arrival of the hunters, machans would be made on three trees on three sides of the village at some distance away from it and a goat would be tied near each tree as bait. Two hunters were assigned for each machan; one for the night shift and the other for the day shift. It was hoped that one of the bleating goats would attract the tiger and be shot from the machan.

This is how Shiv Pratap entered the story. He was an excellent marksman and had hunted deer and wild birds in forests, but tiger hunting was something new for him. He had read all of the books written by Jim Corbett whom he idolized. Reading the stories of the man eaters had made him want to kill one. That is why he had volunteered to be part of the select group.

The tiger entered the Rishi Ghati which is a rectangular valley in Uttara Khand near Himachal Pradesh. It is roughly fifteen kilometers wide and about twice as long. On the east and west there are low hills which become higher towards the north side which has high hills. The valley slopes gently down from the north to the south where it meets the plains region. Two rivers emerge from opposite corners of the northern hills and meet at the center of the southern end of the valley, dividing it into three parts. The triangular region between the two rivers has a small forest and a village.

When the tiger was spotted by the villagers they reported the sighting. A team of six hunters, including Shiv Pratap, was sent to kill it. They met the village headman and a group of other men in the village who told them about the geography of the valley.

One old man said, "Rishi Ghati is protected by a guardian and all our people are safe."

The headman said, "This is a legend which we cannot believe. After the tiger was seen we have brought all our live stock into our homes. I have ordered all persons to remains indoors."

The old man persisted, "The guardian is the spirit of a sadhu who was killed by a tiger in the time of my great grandfather, who told me about it. It is well known that it protects all persons from wild animals. Since that time no person has been killed in Rishi Ghati. That is proof of what I say. We don't need your help. Our guardian will protect everyone."

Several men spoke up against him and said that his brain was senile. Shiv Pratap spoke derisively to the old man, "You can retire your guardian because we have come to get rid of the man eater."

His words stung the old man who said, "Son, you make fun of me, but before you leave this valley, you will surely believe what I say."

At that time Shiv Pratap did not know that soon he would have the strangest experience of his life. After the machans were erected, the hunters took turns to man them. Shiv had preferred the night shift. It was his second night on the machan. So far the man-eater had not approached any of the machans, but the radio collar tracker had confirmed that it was in the valley. All hunters were sure that hunger would soon force it to attack one of the goats.

The goat tied near Shiv became restless and bleated loudly. He was sure that the tiger was nearby. It emerged in the clearing and moved towards the goat. The bright moonlight made it clearly visible. He decided to shoot the tiger before it harmed the goat. He aimed for the tiger's head and squeezed the trigger. The tiger fell and lay still.

Shiv watched it for over ten minutes, but saw no signs of movement. He was certain that the tiger was dead and was about to signal the kill by firing three shot in quick succession. Then he hesitated and decided to climb down and make sure. Prudence dictated that he put a couple of shots into the tiger's chest, but it did not occur to Shiv. He used the rifle strap to sling it on his shoulder and climbed down and stumbled on an exposed root and fell with a loud sound. At that instant the tiger got up and limped towards him. He watched in terror, unable to reach his rifle, which was stuck under him? His whole life flashed before him, and when the tiger was about to pounce, he remembered the words of the old man.

The tiger pounced from about ten feet. Shiv felt himself being lifted up and floating through the air and landing gently on the machan. At first he thought that he was hallucinating and in reality the tiger had killed him. He was thankful that his death did not cause him pain. Within a few seconds he realized that he was on the machan alive and the tiger was climbing the tree. He got hold of his rifle and waited to shoot the animal as soon as he could get a good shot.

That chance came when the tiger climbed from the trunk to his branch. He let him have a shot in the chest. The tiger let out a loud growl and froze in position for a few seconds, which seemed like an eternity to Shiv. Then it slowly tilted to one side and fell to the ground. He shot it twicemore to make sure and gave the pre-arranged signal.

It took some time for the other hunters and the villagers to reach there. They all congratulated him and there was much joyous shouting and firing of guns and rifles. The next day there was a puja at the local temple and a feast in honor of the hunters who were all garlanded. Shiv Pratap was given special treatment, being the man who slew the beast. Many villagers came to touch his feet and bless him.

The old man also came to him and embracing him whispered in his ear, "You must thank the guardian. He saved your life by lifting you to the machan."

Shiv Pratap was stunned. He had not told anyone about being lifted up and placed on the machan, as if by magic. How could the old man have known about it? Was the man a psychic? These questions would puzzle him for the rest of his life. Shiv whispered back, "I agree with you."

Later he reasoned that when he first shot the tiger, the bullet had hit the skull at an acute angle and bounced off. The impact must have concussed the tiger. It was by chance that the tiger regained consciousness at the same instant that he fell. Surely he must have climbed up to the machan, while the tiger came towards him. In his state of terror he must have imaged that a supernatural being had lifted him up, and then placed him on the machan. This explanation was the best he could think of, but it had a flaw. How did the old know that he had imagined being lifted up?

After the feast he went to the temple to offer his prayers and thanked the guardian for saving him, but he was not sure of the truth. Till the end of his life he couldn't decide whether the Guardian saved him or he saved himself.

****

The Hidden Message

Tejas and Vinod joined the BSc course at Allahabad in 1955, and shared the same hostel room for four years. Thus began a close friendship between two contrasting persons.

Tejas was tall and robust, a keen sportsman and an extrovert. He came from a landowning family of Dehradoon, and wanted to join the civil services as an officer, not the IAS but the IPS. He looked upon the former as a cadre of desk bound administrators, while the latter were like knights in shining armor jousting with criminals to bring them to justice.

Vinod was slim and of a thoughtful bent of mind, keenly interested in studies and research, his interest in games being confined to listening to cricket commentaries. He dreamt of becoming a professor of chemistry and discovering new chemicals. His father was a school teacher, and a part time journalist and writer in Saharanpur.

After completing their BSc together, they went on to complete MSc in chemistry. Later Vinod enrolled for a PhD, while Tejas qualified for the IPS. The two friends were sorry to be parted and promised to keep in touch.

His training over, Tejas was posted as an ASP at Saharanpur District, where he reported to the SSP, who welcomed him and said, "I am happy to get a bright young officer, but you are totally raw and untested. Don't let the power and prestige of your position go to your head. Remember we are the servants of the people."

"Yes sir," Tejas responded.

The SSP continued, "Report to Mr. Ravi Kumar, the SP, who holds the overall charge of the city areas of Saharanpur, Roorkee and Hardwar. You will look after the Saharanpur city area, under his guidance. Think of yourself as a trainee attached to him." Tejas nodded his head in agreement and the SSP continued. "Opium is being smuggled from Pakistan to Delhi via Kashmir, Himachal and

Saharanpur. That is because many consignments were intercepted by the police in Punjab and Rajasthan, so the smugglers have started using this new route. Mr. Ravi Kumar has assigned a CID inspector to gather information from underworld sources. From today you will be in charge. We want to discover the king-pins on this route. This task will take priority over your other duties, which are of a routine nature. Maintain secrecy, and don't initiate any action against the smugglers without clearance from Mr. Ravi Kumar."

Tejas reported to Mr. Ravi Kumar, a tall man in his late thirties. He told Tejas that the CID Inspector had not been able to gather any information. Either the local petty criminals did not know anything, or they were afraid to talk to the police. Tejas thought quickly, and came up with the idea of using CID men, who would work under cover posing as recently released convicts. Two men were transferred from Lucknow, and placed at his disposal.

Tejas had written to Vinod about his posting. Soon he got a reply urging him to visit Vinod's father, Mr. Brij Verma. He visited him that very day. Mr. Verma, a widower, lived in a small rented house on the outskirts of the city. There were ploughed fields across the road from the house. Behind it was a small field covered with trees. The nearest house was more than a hundred yards away. Leaving his driver and constable with the official jeep, Tejas walked through the open boundary gate, and knocked on the front door. It was opened by Mr. Verma who said, "You must be Tejas. Vinod talks and writes so much about you, that I feel that I have known you for years."

They entered the sitting room, and sat on wooden chairs, sipping tea made by Devi Prasad, the part time servant. Mr. Verma was a lean and unassuming person, dressed in white khadi pajama and kurta. The sitting room had a desk, a few chairs, a small table and a large number of wooden racks, stacked with books. They talked about Tejas's work, Vinod's research, and Mr. Verma's journalistic work and his writings. He promised to gift Tejas his book, describing his experiences during the freedom movement. Tejas spoke about the opium smuggling, cautioning him not to mention it to anyone. He also felt that the house was unsafe, particularly with the old man being alone at night. He said as much.

Mr. Verma replied, "You police officers are overly security conscious. I have little money and no enemies. Books are my only wealth. Why would a thief come here?"

While leaving Tejas said, "You are like a father to me. If there is anything I can do for you, please don't hesitate to ask."

Mr. Verma responded, "I also feel that you are like a son to me. In a few days I will invite you for dinner, but feel free to visit whenever you like."

Little did Tejas realize that his visit would trigger a chain of tragic events?

Each day Tejas would spend about an hour or two, in the morning and afternoon, attending to his office. At other times he would go to visit the police posts. Each day he would park his jeep at a different place in some crowded market. One of his undercover CID men would pass by, and secretly drop a crumpled paper message into his jeep. These men also had access to a phone to contact his office if something came up suddenly.

After two weeks, Devi Prasad delivered Mr. Verma's book in a sealed packet and left a verbal message with the duty clerk at Tejas's office, inviting him for dinner at Mr. Verma's house the next night. He also insisted that, "Tejas sahib must open the cover and read what is written at the back as soon as he returns, and send acceptance for dinner to my sahib tomorrow morning at his school."

Tejas immediately opened the packet, which contained the book. It was a hardbound edition with a glazed paper cover. On the back was a poem by Mr. Verma in honor of Gandhiji, which Tejas read immediately. Little did he realize that Mr. Verma had written a message on the inside of the cover, which was the one intended for him.

Later that night he read the book. He was moved by the pain and suffering that Mr. Verma had endured during the freedom struggle, when he was hand cuffed, beaten with canes and thrown into prison, where he spent six months, and was dismissed from his government job. He then found a job as an English teacher in a private school.

The next morning Tejas sent a note to Mr. Verma, informing that he would reach his house for dinner at seven thirty in the evening. His jeep reached the house a couple of minutes before seven thirty. It was dark, but the lights were not on. His knocking produced no response. The driver and constable accompanied him to the back of the house. They entered the dining room through an open door and switched the light on. Through the kitchen door, they could see the cooking utensils on the coal fire, with the food burnt. They entered the sitting room through another door. Switching on the light, they saw Mr. Verma lying in a pool of blood, with his throat slit. The overturned furniture showed that a fierce struggle had taken place.

Tejas was overcome by emotion, but controlled himself to recover quickly, to perform his duty as a police officer. He held Mr. Verma's wrist. There was no pulse. A quick search of the premises revealed no sign of Devi Prasad or any obvious clue. There was much to do: an immediate search for the murderers, the arrangement for the postmortem and sending messages to Vinod at Allahabad and his uncles who resided at Meerut.

They arrived the next day, while Vinod came a day later. Tejas's heart quailed at the thought of meeting his best friend, whose father was murdered under his very nose. He tried to console Vinod as best as he could, and promised that he would ensure that justice was done. Even several months of investigations failed to provide any answers in the case. There was no trace of Devi Prasad. His home was in a nearby village, but he had not returned home.

There was better progress in the opium smuggling investigations. The opium kingpin was identified as, Puran Chand alias Mota Seth, a man who owned an auto repair workshop and a truck business. A big consignment of opium was expected to arrive from Kashmir via Himachal by a car carrying a young couple dressed as a bride and groom. The car would drop the couple at a rented house, decorated to receive them, and then proceed to the workshop where the opium would be transferred to a secret compartment of a truck. It would later be loaded with goods to be transported to Delhi.

Tejas thought that Mota Seth must know the names of the kingpins in Himachal and Delhi. Why not use him to catch them also?

Accordingly, he approached Mr. Ravi Kumar, who said, "We must coordinate with the Himachal and Delhi police." The two met the SSP who said, "Mota Seth will cooperate if we promise to arrange a lenient sentence for him. I will happily approve that, provided you catch the kingpins of Kashmir, Himachal and Delhi also."

Tejas planned the operation accordingly. His men, dressed in plain clothes, were placed to watch Mota Seth's house, his garage, the rented house meant to receive the bridal couple and the approach route of the car. His phones were tapped and one particular conversation gave the exact date of arrival of the opium consignment.

On that date, the car arrived, late in the afternoon, and dropped the bridal couple at the decorated house before proceeding to the workshop. Every move was reported to Tejas. His men were alert to intercept the smugglers if they tried to take the opium out of the city. Just after dark one of his men cut Mota Seth's phone line and Tejas entered the house with a few men to arrest him. A servant received them and went to summon his master. Soon they heard a commotion. Mota Seth, who had tried to sneak out through the back door, was brought inside struggling and protesting loudly, "You will pay heavily for arresting an innocent man."

Tejas rebuked him, "Will an innocent man try to escape? We have your car, your truck, your opium and even the fake bride and groom and all of your men. I will make sure that you get the maximum possible jail sentence."

The color drained from the man's face and he whimpered, "Sahib, how can you benefit by sending me to jail? If you let me go, I will make you rich. You can even arrest all of my men with the opium and get credit for the case, but please let me escape."

Tejas told him firmly, "Give me the names and addresses of the kingpins in Kashmir, Himachal and Delhi now. We will arrest them, and you must give evidence against them. Then my senior officers will request the court to give you a lenient sentence."

Mota Seth agreed and kept his side of the bargain. The operation was a complete success. The kingpins of Kashmir, Himachal and Delhi and their men were convicted and awarded the maximum sentences, while Mota Seth and his gang received lesser ones. Tejas was awarded a medal, and the others involved received commendations.

Twenty years passed by, Tejas was stationed in Lucknow as a DIG. His old SP, Mr. Ravi Kumar, was the DG in charge of police in UP. One day Tejas decided to read Mr. Verma's book once more. While removing it from the self, the outer cover got torn, revealing a message written by Mr. Verma and addressed to Tejas. The relevant portion is reproduced below.

"A stranger, named Satish, had seen your jeep parked outside my house when you visited me. After much hesitation, he approached me today because he is afraid to go to the police directly. He will be present at my house when you come for dinner, and will give information about his boss, who is an opium smuggler. In return he wants a reward and pardon. Please confirm the invitation."

As Tejas read the message, he remembered Devi Prasad's instructions which he had misunderstood. He had read the poem instead of the hidden message. Fate had played a very cruel trick. In a flash his mind solved the murder mystery. It was certainly a triple murder. Mota Seth's men had seen Satish, visiting Mr. Verma's house in a furtive manner. Mota Seth had him tortured till he revealed all, after which he was killed and buried in some secluded spot. Then Mota Seth sent his men to kill Brij Verma, before Tejas arrived at his house. On hearing Mr. Verma's screams, Devi Prasad rushed from the kitchen, leaving the food on the fire. He struggled with the assailants, but seeing his master lying dead and fearing for his own life, he ran out through the back door. The assailants chased him, and caught and killed him at some distance from the house. They dared not return to the house for fear of Tejas having reached there. Then they carried away Devi Prasad's body to bury it. Clearly, Mota Seth was responsible for three murders and disposing of two of the bodies. Tejas resolved that he would bring him and his men to justice. He wrote a letter to Vinod part of which is given below:

"I have discovered a clue which will help me bring your father's murderers to justice. This in no way reduces the sorrow, that I will always feel, for not being able to prevent his death. No matter how long it takes, I will catch the criminals and bring them to justice. The clue has given me a hint of who could be involved. I will be busy with the investigation and will visit you in a few days when I find the time."

He met Mr. Ravi Kumar with the message, and his reconstruction of the events. The latter agreed with him and said, "After so many years it will not be easy to trace the criminals. Some may have died, but you must pursue the case for the sake of justice. I will relieve you from your other duties."

Tejas sent a CID team to Saharanpur to start the investigation in a secretive manner, and he traveled to Saharanpur, stopping at Roorkee where his friend Vinod was now a Professor. It was an emotional reunion. Tejas explained every detail to him, and proceeded to Saharanpur to guide his men. Soon his men discovered that Mota Seth had shifted to Bahraich along with some of his former assistants. They had adopted new identities, and were smuggling electronics goods and woolens from China via Nepal.

Now the question arose, how to prove the charges against the killers? There was no proof that Devi Prasad and Satish had been murdered. If only their bodies could be found and identified? The only eye witnesses were Mota Seth's own men. He must offer lenient terms to some of them, to use them as witnesses against their boss and the men who had committed the murders. Still it would be a herculean task to prove the case in court.

Tejas pondered the matter. He instructed his men to discover who among Mota Seth's men could have been the killers. Two of his men remained in Saharanpur and the others proceeded to Bahraich. The suspicion zeroed in on two brothers, Girdhari and Birju. They were powerfully built men who generally enforced discipline in the gang of smugglers.

Having decided his further course of action, he went to Bahraich, arrested the entire gang on the charges of Mr. Verma's murder and smuggling, and shifted them to Saharanpur for interrogation. Mota Seth, Girdhari and Birju were placed in solitary cells, away from the others. Tejas applied his entire knowledge and experience to conduct a skillful interrogation to extract vital information regarding the burial points of the bodies. The decomposed bodies were exhumed and identified- Satish's by a metal front tooth and Devi Prasad's by his copper amulet. Now the charge was triple murder and smuggling.

This breakthrough enabled him to extend the period of custody of the criminals. Using this time effectively for further interrogations and investigations, he prepared a fool proof case, consisting of over a thousand pages of confessional statements, tests results, forensic reports and photos. It contained a detailed reconstruction of the three murders, and identified the role of each criminal involved. It was authentic because he had taken the criminals to the murder and burial sites several times to verify every event.

He made sure that he was present on every day of the trial which lasted many months. He guided the public prosecutor in a skillful manner so that the court had no hesitation in awarding life sentences to Mota Seth, Girdhari and Birju; while the rest received varying sentences depending on their crimes, and how much they had cooperated with the police.

Vinod was deeply touched by his friend's sincere efforts. Tejas was greatly satisfied that the message had ensured that justice was done, and the promise made to his friend was fulfilled.

****

Tales and Trivia from Academia I

Introduction: The purpose of these tales is to give a human touch to academia and not to tarnish its image. Some of these tales may be based on events which might have occurred long ago, but most of them are purely imaginary. Some are intended to be funny while others give glimpses of mundane events in the lives of students and teachers.

Having made this point clear, it is also necessary to state that academia includes the highest academic universities as well as colleges and even the schools. The reader may wonder why many of the tales are related to IITs and are biased in favor of engineers and why they have the flavor of the 1960ies. This is because of the author's IIT and engineering student background of those good old days of the 60ies.

Ragging At IIT: Ragging has a long history, which goes back several centuries to schools in England. It was frowned upon by the authorities, who tried to ensure that it did not cross the limits of decency and there was no violence or injury. The old students established dominance over the new students who were called freshers. They made fun of them in various different ways by giving them silly tasks. The ragging period used to last for a couple of weeks and would end with a mass ragging on a night in which all freshers were assembled at one place in the open and some sort of initiation ceremonies were held. After that night, ragging would end.

Where new students were allotted rooms in the same hostel as the old students, it was impossible to escape from being ragged. Nobody enjoyed being ragged and it was something which most new students tolerated. They would be asked silly questions, made to sing, dance, crawl under a bed, climb on to a cupboard or made to run or hop for a long time. It was best to readily do what was asked. However some new students would resist by acting tough or smart. These were subjected to severe ragging which would last for a very long time. Some students were a bit more sensitive and were upset by even the mildest ragging and would run away to their homes. They would exaggerate the ragging to their parents to justify their running away and some parents would believe every word of what they said.

A peculiar case of ragging concerns a particularly sensitive and innocent student, who ran away to his home and was promptly sent back, accompanied by his uncle and elder brother. They stayed with him for several days in his hostel room and accompanied him everywhere including the dining hall and would even escort him to the class room and wait outside to bring him back. They went back after the ragging was over, but he still wanted to go back home. It took the best efforts of his class mates to dissuade him from leaving IIT permanently.

He told his friends that he was from a small village and was the first person from it to be selected in an IIT. It was a great honor for his village. Almost the entire village accompanied him to the railway station where he was garlanded by several of the village elders.

He had no idea about the ragging that awaited him at his hostel. In his innocence he assumed that a grand reception awaited all new students. He thought that the Director and Faculty would welcome the new students with a grand ceremony and speeches in their honor. Instead, to his shock and horror, he faced ragging as soon as he reached the hostel. The unfortunate part was that there were no other freshers being ragged along with him and he ran away as soon as he could. If he had met some other freshers, they would have explained to him about ragging and dissuaded him from running away. All's well that ends well. In due course of time he adjusted very well with life in the hostel and the engineering studies in which he excelled.

And Who Are You? A few days after the ragging was over, a Fresher's Function was held in the IIT Auditorium to introduce them individually on the stage by name, branch and hall of residence. A variety entertainment program was organized in which the talented new students participated. They presented well rehearsed items comprising songs, dances, instrumental music and skits.

The best item was a song by a rather attractive girl named RXY, who sang in an extremely melodious voice. Later a new boy named PNQ bragged to some of his class mates that he had been introduced to her and would introduce them to her. A group of them met her when she was on her way to attend classes. PNQ stopped her and introduced his friends.

RXY smiled and said, “Now that you have introduced them, could you kindly tell me who are you?” After that PNQ became the target of many jokes and much teasing.

Kharagpurvasla Etcetera: During the 1960ies I was studying in the third year at IIT Kharagpur and had come home for the Durga Puja vacations. An old friend of my father came to visit us and my father introduced me to him. Our conversation was as follows: He said, “So you are studying Civil Engg at Kharagpurvasla.”

This startled me. It is well known that Kharagpur is a town in Bengal which is home to the country's first IIT, while Khadakvasla is home to the NDA of the armed forces. This merging of the identities of these two towns into one came as a big shock. I felt that if I pointed out his mistake, he might feel embarrassed so I nodded my head vaguely.

He continued, “Have you started using the slide rule for making drawings?” This was another big blunder. A t-square along with set squares etcetera was used for drawing, while a slide rule was an instrument used by engineers for calculations. The advent of the calculator made it obsolete. Again I had no answer to his question.

Then he asked, “Now that you are in third year, can you design and construct a small house?” The question was rather odd and again revealed his ignorance of Engg studies. During the first three years we covered Physics, Chemistry, Mathematics, Humanities, Surveying and Drawing etcetera. The subjects of Concrete, Steel and Masonry Design, Foundation Engineering etcetera, essential for building design, were covered later in the 4th and 5th years.

When I answered in the negative, he was shocked and said, “You are in the third year and they have taught you nothing about engineering.”

Extending his reasoning to medical education, a third year MBBS student should be competent to treat sick children and carry out operations on them.

At that time I was appalled by his ignorance, but now I think I judged him too harshly. Today, when I talk with young people about their studies or profession, I find myself to be ignorant of what they are studying or doing. Probably their opinion about me is the same as mine was about my father's friend.

Topo: Many years ago engineering students were overloaded with huge quantities of home work. Most students would copy much from what others did or from assignments of previous batches of students. Glass plate topo was used for tracing drawings and diagrams. This required a glass plate supported at its four corners on stacks of books with a table lamp under it. The drawing was placed on the glass plate and a paper would be placed on the drawing. On switching the lamp the drawing would be clearly visible and could be traced easily.

Profs generally ignored the copying. On rare occasions they took action against the copiers. Those who copied generally got better marks because their work was neat and tidy. Once, a teacher reported a group of students to the Head of Department for copying some tutorial problems. They were asked to submit written apologies. One of them wrote his apology and the rest copied it word for word and they were all accepted without any objection.

Another time four students made copies of an old drawing using glass plate topo. The drawing had a mistake. At one place a beam was labeled as 'Jup Beam'. Three of the students copied it as such, while the fourth saw the mistake and correctly labeled it as 'Top Beam'. The three were asked to explain the meaning of 'Jup Beam', and were scolded for copying. The teacher assumed that the fourth one had made the drawing and the others had copied it and made the mistake while copying. He was scolded for allowing the others to copy his work.

Workshop practical reports were submitted in files covers. One person submitted an old file of a senior batch which had over twenty pages. It had been signed by the Prof on the last page. He copied that page and replaced it and the cover while retaining all of the old pages. The teacher scolded him, "In future please write the complete report by yourself and do not submit one page written by someone else."

In modern times copying is no longer known as TOPO because now the 'copy' and `paste' commands have become legitimate tools. These are used even for copying research papers and thesis. Soon most humans may not need to use pen, paper, or the brain because AI will write letters, reports, research papers etcetera in response to voice commands. In the future, even research might be conducted by AI with little or no human intervention. One shudders to think that the human brain might shrink to the size of a pea after generations of disuse.

****

How Water and Life Arrived on Earth

Billions of years ago, the Earth was a lifeless, barren desert. Violent storms lasted for months and raised clouds of dust far greater than any in the Sahara of today. Even the sand dunes dwarfed those of today. At some point of time, some momentous events on Jupiter triggered a series of actions which brought water and life to the earth, while the former became devoid of life. One planet's loss became the other planet's gain.

It is a rather long story, but can be condensed by skipping the insignificant details. Billions of years ago, Jupiter was teeming with life. It had vast oceans populated by numerous creatures of various species having diverse, shapes and sizes. The land areas were immense, with forests, deserts, coastal areas and mountains. The land life was as abundant and as varied as the marine life and included far more varieties of animals, birds, mammals, insects, reptiles, plants, fungi and bacteria than our present day Earth.

Among the animals, was a creature which became the cause of Jupiter's down fall. This being, which had more brains than other animals, struggled to gain dominance over all others. It gradually adopted a bipedal stance, learned to make tools and use fire. It progressed through various stages of civilization- hunter gatherer, farmer and city dweller. With further development of religion, social living, politics, arts, medicine, science and technology, these beings organized themselves into nationalities which warred with each other. In short they were very similar to humans.

Soon they learned about the futility of war and started to live in relative peace, as a federation of nations. All this while, their science and technology made far more rapid progress than other disciplines. In a few hundred generations, they transformed from simple god fearing beings into arrogant believers in science and its ability to solve the problems created by their industrial progress. Soon science and technology became their new religion.

At some stage they faced the problem of global warming. Polar ice and glaciers started melting at an alarming rate, causing sea levels to rise. Their scientists and technologists worked feverishly to develop technologies and techniques to reduce global warming, but the problem could not be solved overnight. It would take time. In the meantime vast coastal areas become submerged and many people had to move to already overcrowded higher areas.

Worse still, many coastal resorts and casinos had closed down. Some others survived by constructing protective dykes as in Holland. These were very costly and their level had to be raised frequently due to rising sea levels. The tourism and gambling industries had big clout with political parties. They lobbied and applied pressure to find a quick solution to the problem.

The Secretary General of their federation appointed a think tank of leading scientists and technologists to solve the problem. The think tank made extensive use of AI to come up with a brilliant solution to stop further submergence. They decided to pump vast quantities of water from the oceans and send it into space. This would maintain the oceans at the present level and buy them time to develop technologies to effectively control global warming.

They needed a vast quantity of energy to pump the water and send it into space. All of their nuclear plants were harnessed together to produce sufficient energy to power a few gigantic pumps. Force fields were created in the form of vertical tubes stretching millions of miles from the oceans into space. The pumps were provided with filters made of electronic force fields which would prevent living beings from being pumped out with the water.

This operation was inaugurated by the Secretary General and was a grand success. The pumps sent water through the force field tubes millions of miles away from Jupiter and out of its gravitational field. The ocean levels started subsiding gradually and some submerged areas were recovered. There was much jubilation over the entire planet.

Alas, this was short lived. One of the nuclear reactors overheated, causing the others to do the same. The nuclear reactions proceeded at an ever faster rate, pumping out water at a faster rate till finally the chain reaction went out of control. All of the reactors exploded one after the other causing catastrophic damage and loss of life and huge secondary explosions and fires which lasted for years. This holocaust finally destroyed all life and even its traces were wiped out.

Much water had gone into space. A huge quantity coalesced and was pulled in the direction of the sun. On its way it slammed into the earth and remained there to form it oceans. Some water either coalesced on floating meteors and formed vast numbers of comets or went to Mars and Venus. This water did not have any life forms, which had been blocked by the electronic filters. However it carried the basic molecules which are the building blocks of life.

As fate would have it, the conditions in the earth's new oceans were ideal for the development of life from the basic molecules. It was a long and slow process for life to develop and it took us billions of years to reach the present stage of civilization. Let us hope we do not become arrogant like the people of Jupiter and meet a similar fate.

Many may doubt this story. However, space missions are becoming increasingly sophisticated and their reach is extending further and further. Who knows, that one day Jupiter may be explored by some mission, which might find some traces of its once mighty civilization.

****

The Legend of Asha Lata and Vikram

Avyan and Vimal had planned a weekend outing to the hill resort at Jamtal, a nice little town nestled in the lower Himalayas. It would be cool, a welcome relief from the heat of the plains. The place had a wonderful ambience with many old British era buildings with their sloping roofs all well maintained. Even the new construction blended with the old, unlike some other hill resorts, whose beauty was marred by the jarring contrast between the old and the new.

The scenic beauty, the winding walking paths near the lake, the sound of wind blowing through the pine trees, the neat market place with its shops and restaurants were all to his liking. Best of all was the hotel where they would be staying. Its core was an old wooden bungalow to which several new rooms had been added. The service was excellent and the food was delicious.

Their last visit had been wonderful. Vimal had felt rejuvenated, a feeling which had lasted many weeks, but now after the daily grind he had been feeling rather low in spirits.

Avyan suggested a second visit. He had said, "This time the trip will be even better because of the interesting company. My boss Mr. Ashok Verma and his wife will stay at our hotel."

The idea of spending time with a couple, who were probably of middle age with old fashioned ideas, did not appeal to Vimal. He thought that Avyan would most likely be busy trying to please his boss.

He snorted loudly and said, "You will be trying to butter your boss all the time and expect me to do the same."

"No, he is more like a friend and there will definitely be someone whom you will like," he replied in a persuasive tone.

"Who?" Vimal asked.

"Let it be a surprise," is all he said.

On the eve of the trip, Vimal had dinner alone at the rooms they shared, because Avyan had to work late to finish some urgent office work. Vimal's thoughts drifted to his recent past. His parents had passed away one after the other a few years ago and he had no siblings. The love showered on him by his aunts and uncles sustained him and the pressure of work did not leave time for self pity.

The aunts would say, "Poor boy, he is so lonely. We must find a nice girl for him."

Almost every month they would come up with a new proposal and arrange meetings with girls. He liked two of these but each time he heard a woman's voice in his mind which prevented him from giving his consent. A loud thunder clap brought an end to his thoughts and the welcome sound of rain prompted him to step out on the balcony and extend his arm to let a few rain drops fall on his hand. Soon the rain increased and he stepped back into the bedroom. He sat on his bedside chair and started to read a historical novel based on chivalry and romance in the Rajasthan of a thousand years ago.

The hero was the valiant prince Vikram, who led his aged father's armies in battle to defend his kingdom of Amarkot against the two powerful rulers, Raja Kansa of Sherkot and Raja Veersain of Kalgarh whose territories were on the western, northern and eastern borders of Amarkot. Raja Ranjit of Chandanpur on the southern border sent part of his army to aid Vikram. Even though their army was much smaller than the enemy armies, Vikram managed to drive them out. There was rejoicing in Amarkot and bards wrote songs in praise of his valiant deeds and handsome looks. His father passed away and he was crowned king and became renowned for his just and honest rule, arousing the envy of his enemies Kansa and Veersain who were both wicked tyrants.

Kansa had a beautiful daughter, Asha Lata, who was a talented singer and had a sound knowledge of Vedas, Puranas, Ramayana and the Mahabhartha. She was the equal of any pandit in learned discussions and debates. She had heard the bards singing about Vikram's valiant deeds, his sense of justice and his handsome looks, and had secretly fallen in love with him.

Vikram had also heard about her beauty, talent and learning. He commissioned an artist to make a painting based on the bard's songs depicting her beauty and hung it in his bedroom. Secret messages expressing their love were exchanged between the two. Their two kingdoms had been enemies for centuries. There had been many battles between them.

He consulted his ministers who said that it would be wise to have a marriage alliance with Sherkot so that the two kingdoms would be at peace with each other. An emissary was sent to the court of Kansa laden with gifts and a marriage proposal for Asha Lata and a treaty of friendship between their two kingdoms. Kansa had other plans. He coveted Vikram's kingdom. He spurned the offer and had the emissary thrashed, his clothes torn, head tonsured, face blackened and sent him back with a message threatening war and the destruction of Amarkot.

Kansa offered his daughter's hand in marriage to Veersain and asked him to support his proposed invasion of Amarkot. Veersain was much older than Asha Lata and had several wives and children. He immediately accepted the marriage proposal and agreed to support the invasion on the condition that he would get a share in the territory of Vikram. They both started collecting more soldiers for their armies.

Asha Lata had been distressed when Vikram's proposal was spurned and this latest development saddened her even more. Her mother had passed away long ago and she received no support from her step mother and step brother. Her maid and close confidant suggested a ruse by which she could hope to marry Vikram. Asha Lata told her father that she would marry according to his wish, but would first visit the temple in her mother's town for a few days to seek the blessings of the goddess Durga. This temple was near the border of Amarkot.

The maid's husband went to Vikram's court secretly with the message that he should make a surprise raid on the temple during her visit, and capture her. Some of the courtiers suspected that this was a trick to trap Vikram, but they agreed to the plan when the maid's husband offered himself as a hostage. Vikram led the raid and brought Asha Lata safely to Amarkot where their marriage was celebrated with much rejoicing. Ranjit and his courtiers also attended as honored guests and promised to help in case of an attack by Kansa and Veersain.

Kansa was burning with a desire for revenge and asked Veersain to march with him to invade and destroy Amarkot. The latter suggested that their armies should enter the territory of Chandanpur and besiege the capital. This would force Vikram to come to the aid of Chandanpur. At night the armies of Sherkot and Kalgarh would slip quietly out of their camp leaving a skeleton force to deceive the enemy. They would march straight to Amarkot fort and capture it before the deception was discovered. With the fort in their hands they could control the whole state making it difficult for Vikram and Ranjit to retake it.

The ruse worked to the extent that Vikram sent part of his army to Chandanpur. He did not want to leave his new bride at Amarkot with a small garrison to defend it. He suspected an enemy trick, so he himself remained behind with a strong garrison. He also advised his army commander to march back in case the enemy attacked Amarkot. After two days a large enemy force was sighted approaching the fort. Messengers were sent to Chandanpur through a secret tunnel which led from the fort to a forest.

The enemy surrounded the fort and made repeated assaults using ladders to scale the walls. Archers would fire arrows at the defenders on the fort walls. Foot soldiers would carry ladders to be put up against the walls for the attackers to climb. The defenders would shoot arrows at the men carrying the ladders. Once a ladder was rested against the fort wall, boiling oil and red hot gravel would be poured on the men climbing up and also attempts would be made to topple the ladder.

If any of the attackers managed to climb the walls these were dispatched by the defenders. Vikram's skill in managing and motivating his soldiers was essential in repulsing the repeated assaults made by the enemy. After each assault there was a lull but Vikram remained active, supervising the defense, making sure that the fires were burning and oil and gravel were kept hot for the next attack, and the wounded were treated. The assaults continued all day and stopped at night. Several of Vikram's men had been killed or rendered unfit for battle, but the enemy lost far more men. At night Vikram rested, leaving a trusted commander to be vigilant against surprise night attacks.

The next morning the enemy made a fresh attack with a larger number of men. During the night they had cut down many trees and made more ladders. The defenders were stretched to the limit before they could repulse this attack. An enemy soldier had managed to climb the walls and was lying on the battlement pretending to be dead. He got up suddenly and swung his sword at Vikram hitting him on the helmet. The attacker was quickly overpowered but Vikram had been knocked unconscious. He was carried away to his chamber to be treated by a Vaid. Asha Lata was greatly distressed. She knelt down to pray to the goddess Durga. The situation was grave. The defense could not resist more attacks without Vikram's leadership.

The sound of thunder startled Vimal, who had been reading for a long time and his eyes were tired. He put the book down and was concerned that Avyan had not returned because they needed to leave early in the morning. He heard a knock on the door and thought that Avyan had returned. He wondered why Avyan had not used his key and why he had knocked. He switched on the stair case light and peeped through the eyehole.

He saw a beautiful lady in a gold embroidered sari and wearing considerable gold jewelry. She had a mysterious and eerie look. Maybe it was his imagination. The book that he had been reading, the sound of thunder could have helped distort his imagination. Possibly she was a relation of their landlord who lived on the ground floor. Not finding the landlord and his family at home, she may have come up to enquire. Wouldn't he do the same if he visited a friend and found his door locked and the first floor lights switched on? Anyway he was a strong muscular man with nothing to fear from a lady so he opened the door.

Immediately she said, "Vimal you must come with me otherwise the enemy will capture Amarkot."

Her lips had not moved but he heard the words in his mind. It was the same voice which he had heard earlier which had prevented him from giving his consent for the marriage proposals of the two girls he had liked. He was too stunned to reply, but she read his mind and said, "Vikram and Vimal are the same person. He is injured. You must take his place immediately"

Then she grasped his right hand. There was a flash of light and he saw that they were standing on the battlement of a fort, it was morning and he was in medieval armor with a sword in his hand. On seeing them, many soldiers shouted, "Maharaja Vikram ki jai."

Soon there was an assault by the enemy. The defenders went about their duties with vigor and Vimal played the role of Vikram bravely. The attack was repulsed and then many more. He lost count. It was late afternoon when a soldier standing on the lookout tower shouted, "Our armies are approaching under the banner of Maharaja Ranjit."

All the defenders started chanting, "Durga mata ki jai!"

Soon the attackers on the ground saw the approaching army. The weary and disheartened soldiers broke ranks and fled. King Kansa and Veersain and their horsemen could not stop them so they also joined the rout. The defenders had won a great victory, only the follow up remained. Vimal was exhausted, so he sent one of his commanders to request Ranjit to send the army in pursuit of the enemy to capture as many as they could but not indulge in unnecessary slaughter.

A maid came running and led Vimal to a chamber where Asha Lata was waiting. After the maid left Asha Lata said, "Vikram has recovered. He and the real Asha Lata must not see us. Nor should the soldiers see two pairs of Vikram and Asha Lata. You were truly magnificent. Our work is done and we must depart."

This puzzled him, but she grasped his hand and the next instance he found himself in his own bed. Soon he was fast asleep. The next thing he felt was Avyan shaking him and saying, "Wake up. I'll get the car out of the garage. You have five minutes to get ready and come down; else I'll leave without you."

Soon Vimal was in the car mumbling, "Sorry, I am still sleepy. You'll have to drive all the way."

Avyan said, "Still sleepy, but you were fast asleep when I returned."

Vimal slept soundly throughout the journey and woke up only when Avyan shouted, "Come out and let us check into our room."

By now Vimal was wide awake but still felt tired. It was past ten when they sat down for breakfast. Avyan had picked a large table and Vimal was sitting with his back to the entrance.

Avyan whispered, "The interesting company is here," and got up and continued, "Mr. Verma, I hope you all had a pleasant drive. Meet my friend Vimal."

Vimal got up and shook hands with Mr. Verma, who was a slim smart man only slightly older than the two friends.

He said, "Your friend talks a lot about you. Let me introduce everyone. My wife Kamla, her sister Shivani and my sister Nisha and these two are Avyan and Vimal."

Vimal could have sworn that Shivani was Asha Lata in modern attire, the same beautiful face and gorgeous figure. He noticed a brief look of surprise and recognition on her face. Maybe she saw the same look on his face. The others did not notice this. They all had breakfast together. Then Mr. Verma said, "My wife and I will stroll over to the market leaving you four to get better acquainted."

They ordered more coffee and sat chatting for a while and Avyan said to Nisha, "Your legs must be cramped after the long drive. Let me take you for a stroll on a walking path to see the snow covered peaks."

At last, Vimal was alone with Shivani. Their eyes became riveted on each other and there was an incredible chemistry between them. They talked excitedly. After a while she said, "This is my first visit here. Won't you take me for a stroll?"

"There is a nice quiet pathway through the woods," Vimal replied and they headed there. They walked for several minutes enjoying the sights and sounds of nature and conversing like old friends. Several times she addressed him as Vikram and then their conversation went like this.

Vimal, "You got my name wrong. I am Vimal and not Vikram."

Shivani, "Sorry, but you look exactly like him."

Vimal, "Is he a friend of yours?"

Shivani, "No, he was a king and the hero of the book I was reading last night, and you have been constantly addressing me as Asha the heroine of the same book."

Vimal, "I did it unknowingly. I also read the same book and you look exactly like the princess Asha Lata, but there were no pictures in that book. I saw her in my dream and you must also have seen Vikram in a dream."

Shivani, "That was no dream. After Vikram became unconscious, Asha Lata prayed to the goddess Durga and it was she who sent me to take you to the past."

Vimal, "It can't be real. We both read the same book and by chance had similar dreams."

Shivani, "It was real and not a dream. Last night I knocked on your door because the bell was out of order. Then you switched the light on and looked through the peephole and opened the door after much hesitation. I can describe every little detail right from the time that I took you to the past and brought you back holding your hand."

Vimal, "How do you know such details about the visit to our apartment. The visit is not in the book. This defies all scientific logic. Maybe you are psychic or you and I had the same dream."

Shivani, "You men always bring in scientific logic to support your arguments. Why not accept the fact that a thousand years ago you were Vikram and I was Asha Lata."

Vimal, "You are wrong because they are fictional characters."

Shivani, "I am right. You are wrong. The author has stated that his story is based on actual characters and events mentioned in historical documents in the libraries of the former maharajas of Rajasthan."

Vimal held her hand, "let us not argue. I will take you further and show you the wonderful sights."

They went for a long walk holding hands all the while. The weekend passed wonderfully. Avyan and Nisha also got along well. After the trip was over, Vimal and Shivani kept meeting each day. To start with, it was attraction at first sight and then love blossomed. To cut a long story short, they had an early marriage. Avyan and Nisha also got married soon after.

Time passed quickly. Tomorrow is their fifth wedding anniversary. Their romance is still as fresh as it was in the beginning. They agree on most matters but disagree on one. To this day Shivani believes that she was Asha Lata and Vimal was Vikram, but he rejects this.

Now he does not make use of scientific logic to prove her wrong. Instead he says, "You can't be Asha Lata because you are far more beautiful than she was and I can't be Vikram because he was much braver than I am."

Shivani finds it difficult to argue against this logic. Whether events of that night were real or a dream it just does not matter because their life together has been the sweetest dream for them. That is what Nisha and Avyan keep telling them.

****

Tales and Trivia from Academia II

Lunch Time Bath: Water was in short supply at Kharagpur. The hostel bathrooms had running water three times a day- in the morning, during lunch break and the evening for around two hours each time. There simply wasn't enough time for all to bathe in the morning shift, so some preferred the evening time. Both of these shifts were overcrowded. If anyone took more than a couple of minutes for a bath others would start banging on the door of the shower enclosure.

One particular student named APK regularly took a leisurely bath during the lunch hour to avoid the hassle. Others would go straight to the dining hall after classes, but he would go to his room, undress, wrap a towel around his waist, pick up his soap dish, close his door leaving it unlocked and walk along the corridor to the large common bath room which housed the showerand loo enclosures.

Soon his best friends decided to play a trick on him. One of them would quietly pull his towel which hung over the enclosure wall and put it on the hooks near the wash basins. After his bath, APK would discover that the towel was missing. He would shout for the ward boy and ask him for the towel. One fine day, the ward boy was not there. After repeatedly calling him, APK opened the shower door slightly and peered out. There was no one in the bathroom, so he walked to the outer door and peered into the corridor. He found it to be empty and risked a quick dash to his room stark naked. On reaching his room he heaved a sigh of relief and pushed the door open and stepped inside. Imagine his horror when he saw the dhobi (washer man) waiting for him.

The Transistor: Sixty years ago there was no TV broadcast in the country and the main entertainment in the hostel rooms was to listen to music on AIR or Radio Ceylon. Unfortunately radios and transistors were so costly that most students could not afford them. A few enterprising students would buy components from the market and make their own transistors cheaply. Some even sold these to other students to earn some money.

One student SWN bought a home made transistor from a hostel mate RKP and would play it rather loudly at odd hours. The students in the nearby rooms politely requested him to reduce the volume, but he would not do so. Finally one student came up with a solution to this problem. He made a device, which when plugged in a socket, would emit electrical sparks. These created a disturbance which was picked up by the transistor as loud crackling sounds, drowning out the music. He made several such devices which he handed over to his friends in the adjoining rooms.

Next time SWN played the transistor, several of these devices were plugged in. The transistor made such a hideous noise that SWN was forced to switch it off. He rushed with it to RKPs room, complaining that it was defective. RKP switched it on and it played beautiful music with no disturbance. SWN returned to his room and switched it on and again it made the hideous noise.

From then on it was impossible for SWN to listen to music. Instead he got the hideous noise. Repeated trips to RKPs room produced the same result. SWN never suspected the existence of those devices. Some students told him that his room was jinxed. Being a believer in the supernatural, he accepted this explanation and never played his transistor again.

The Difference between Engineers and Doctors: This is a joke in which the engineers and doctors can be substituted by any other two streams of students. Also the position of engineers and doctors can be reversed. It has been told and retold and put in writing countless times. Even so it deserves to be retold here.

Two students from an Engg College and two from the adjacent Medical College went for a weekend visit to a resort. The doctors purchased two rail tickets while the engineers bought only one ticket. The former warned the engineers, "One of you will surely be fined for ticketless travelling."

They boarded the train and sat in the same compartment. When they saw the TTE coming, the two engineers entered the toilet. The TTE knocked on the toilet door and was shown one ticket. He did not realize that there were two persons inside and went away satisfied.

The Doctors having learned the trick bought only one ticket for the return journey. This time the Engineers did not buy any ticket. The Doctors said, "Surely you will be caught this time."

During the journey one of the Engineers shouted, "The TTE is coming."

Both of the doctors entered the toilet. One of the engineers knocked on the door, pretending to be the TTE, and asked for the ticket. One of the doctors opened the door slightly and showed the ticket. The Engineer took it and pocketed it, and went to another compartment with his friend. When the real TTE came, he fined the Doctors for ticketless travelling.

The Difference between Mathematicians and Engineers: This joke is not meant to belittle students of Mathematics. It has been told and retold countless times. It is simply meant to highlight the difference between a theoretician and a practical man. Like the previous joke, it deserves to be included here.

It is said in joke that a Mathematician is a person who is willing to assume anything except responsibility. In reality the truth is that the subject of Mathematics requires rigorous accuracy and proof of correctness. The Engineer, on the other hand, has to use his common sense to get the work done.

During a show the compeer called a Mathematician and an Engineer on to the stage and told them to stand on a line sixteen feet away from a pretty girl. Every time a whistle was blown they could cover half the distance to the girl. The winner would be the person who kissed the girl first.

The whistle was blown and the Engineer walked eight feet towards the girl, but the Mathematician did not move. The compeer asked him why he did not move.

He replied, "The first time I can move eight feet, the second time only four feet and so on. Each time I can move only half of the remaining distance and will never reach the girl even after infinite whistles."

The audience appreciated his logic. The compeer then asked the engineer, "You know you will never be able to cover the distance so why did you move."

The Engineer replied, "After a few whistles, I will get close enough to extend my arms and pull the girl close to me and kiss her."

The audience judged his answer to be better and he was declared as the winner.

I Go: This is a story from an Intermediate College in a small town. During winters the class room was cold. The students would come out and stand in the sun during the time the Physics teacher left and the English teacher arrived. On seeing the teacher the students would rush inside and one particular student used to shout, "I go, I go."

Each time the teacher would say, "This is wrong English. You should say: Let us go."

Little did he realize that the student was speaking in a local dialect of Hindi in which 'I go' meant 'Aa gaya' which translates in English as 'He has come'.

The Whispering Couple: Two close friends used to sit together in class and would frequently whisper to each other. This was a distraction for the class. Most teachers lectured loudly and did not hear their whispers, but a particular teacher was easily distracted. On detecting the source of the disturbance he made them sit at two diagonally opposite corners of the class. One student recited a line of a popular film song, 'Do hanson ka jodabichadgaya.' (A pair of swans has been separated). This elicited laughter and even the teacher smiled.

The Fire Cracker: The lecture was over. The Prof and students walked out of the room. One student remained behind. He took out a fire cracker from his pocket and fixed it to the underside of the teacher's chair using scotch tape. He had previously tied a piece of thick cord to the fuse. Now he lit the cord and blew out the flame. The cord was smoldering slowly with only a slight wisp of smoke. He hurried out of the room before the students of another class started entering the room.

Soon their Prof arrived and took the roll call and started the lecture. After a few minutes the fire reached the fuse which ignited and the cracker went off with a loud bang, magnified by being confined by the class room walls. The Prof and the entire class jumped in fright.

He was a rather strict Prof and known for his harshness. He was incensed and started scolding the class loudly. He refused to accept their explanation that the fire cracker had been placed by a student from the previous class.

He said, "A fire cracker takes only a few seconds to explode. It won't wait for five minutes to explode." He threatened, that unless the guilty student confessed, he would set very difficult test and exam papers to ensure that they all got poor grades. This upset the class.

That afternoon one student went to the Prof's office and said, "Sir, I had put the fire cracker. Please give me whatever punishment you think I deserve, but please spare my class mates. None of them knew about it."

He did not tell any of his class mates about it even though he was upset and worried about his own fate. The next day the Prof came to their class and asked the student to stand up and said, "I am happy that you have confessed. Now I will not take any action against the class. I will also not take any action against you because of your honest confession."

Everyone felt great relief, particularly that courageous student. He had earned the gratitude and respect of his class-mates.

****

The Tug of War

It was the silver jubilee reunion of the 1975 batch of engineers. They were mailed invitation cards to attend the functions in their honor on the occasion of the college convocation. Fittingly the envelopes had a silver border and the invitations were printed on bright blue paper in silver letters. Those who could attend gladly accepted the invitations. It was a great opportunity to meet old friends, revive old memories, and visit the campus where they had spent some of the best years of their lives.

Ravi, Ashok, Vinod and Narendra were among those who accepted the invitations and confirmed their requirements for adjacent rooms in the college guest house. This group of old friends had been inseparable during their student days. They were a lively bunch who had been involved in numerous escapades and brawls, some even involving disciplinary action, but were now settled in life as senior and responsible engineers. Though each was busy in his own life they had maintained contact with each other by phone or letter.

It was a happy group of friends who met at their alma mater. They had brought their families. After the introductions there was much talk about the good old days. The ladies also joined in. There was a tea party and a reception in their honor where they met other old friends. Afterwards they took their families on a walking trip of the campus. Ravi, Ashok and Narendra had been good athletes and had won many medals in their college days. A visit to the college stadium was a must. There was a pleasant breeze and they sat on the stadium benches talking about the medals won and those that had slipped away.

Vinod had never taken part in athletics, but had always gone along to cheer his friends and place bets. Soon the topic drifted to the ladies tug of war. Now he hogged the conversation which had so far been dominated by the other three. The basic story is as narrated by him, barring some minor additions and alterations by the others. However it is essential to explain the rules and basics of tug of war.

A tug of war contest between the Profs and the students was an essential and popular fixture of the annual athletics meet. When the friends were in their first year, the ladies tug of war was introduced. The idea originated from the fertile mind of Mr. Nand Kumar, the Head Coach. He had held this position in a temporary capacity for several years and was hoping to be made regular. He went around coaxing the wives of the senior Profs to participate in a tug of war against the girl students. After much coaxing by him and the junior coaches and a great show of reluctance on their part, the ladies agreed.

The Profs versus the student's tug of war was always the last event and everyone looked forward to it. This time it would be followed by the ladies event. Each team has ten members including one anchor. Generally the anchor is the stoutest person and he stands last in the line of pullers. The end of the rope is passed over his shoulder and looped around his waist. His role is to dig his feet in and act as the anchor while the other nine stand in front of him at regular intervals gripping the rope. The other team stands on the opposite side at some distance. Three equally spaced white lines are marked on the ground between the two teams. A red cloth band is tied on the rope and centered above the central white line. The start is signaled by blowing a whistle. Each side starts pulling the other team towards itself. A team wins a tie if it pulls the other side so that the red cloth band crosses over the white lines on its side. Then the teams change ends for the second tie. The contest is over when a team wins two ties.

To the uninitiated, it may appear that shear weight and brute strength would decide the winner. Experts know that this is only partly true. This sport, like any other, involves considerable skill and tactics, though undoubtedly weight and strength do play a part. Using the right tactics, a light weight team can defeat a heavier and stronger team. At the start, each member of the weaker team should lean back and press their heels into the ground and offer passive resistance. The other side has to exert considerable force and spend energy to pull them because their heels provide high drag resistance. Soon the team which is pulling gets tired, because it takes much energy to pull even a few inches. It is crucial for the captain of the resisting team to judge when the other team is exhausted. He then gives the signal and his team changes posture and starts pulling in earnest and may win if the other team does not react effectively. If at this stage, the other team also changes posture and leans back to offer passive resistance, then the contest may last much longer.

The Profs versus the students contest was one such display of skill and tactics. The former were stronger and heavier and had a good idea of the tactics to be used but lacked in stamina. The latter were lighter but had the advantage of youth. They had considerable practice during the student's interclass tug of war. In the contest the students went into passive mode right from the start. The Profs struggled hard and kept pulling the students gradually inch by inch.

This went on for five minutes and the excitement mounted. The whole crowd of students was cheering for its team in the hope that they would soon tire out the Profs and then pull them over. No such thing happened. Finally an exhausted Profs' team won the tie. This was all pure drama because each year Mr. Kumar used to tell the students to let the Profs win the first tie.

The second tie started off well with both sides simply offering passive resistance. The Profs were too exhausted to pull effectively. The students also just hung on as they wanted to tire out the Profs even more before making their move. When the captain of the student's team saw that the Profs had no energy left, he signaled for his team to start pulling in earnest and the contest was over in a few seconds. The contest stood at one all.

This is how the contest had fared in all previous years. Now as per past tradition there was a short break. The Profs conferred and their captain went to the mike and announced that his team was exhausted and wanted to concede victory to the student team. There was loud cheering from the assembled student crowd. Then the student team captain took the mike and praised the Profs for their valiant effort and said that they did not deserve to lose and so both teams should be joint winners.In response the crowd gave a thunderous roar of approval. The same scene had been repeated in all previous years as far back as anyone could remember.

As per tradition, there had been considerable betting among first year boys on the outcome. The seniors as a rule did not bet. Opinions were evenly divided and many bets were placed for and against the students winning. Vinod was the odd man out. He was the only one who predicted a draw. He was aware of past traditions because he had some inside info. The others mostly were not aware of the tradition. Being mathematically minded, they reasoned that a draw was possible only if there were an even number of contests, but not in case of three which is an odd number. The drawn result ensured that Vinod pocketed a tidy sum of money.

Now the stage was set for the ladies tug of war. Here there were no past traditions. It was all new ground. Whatever happened on the day might set traditions for the future. Since both sides were new to the contest, Mr. Kumar and the other coaches had to explain the rules and tactics to the two teams. On one side were the girls in their sports gear of running shoes and sleeveless vests. Most of the girls were slim and athletically built, weighing between forty five to sixty kg. Only the anchor was slightly heavier and more muscular, being the shot-putt and hammer throw champion.

On the other side were the ladies dressed in their colorful saris and blouses with lots of makeup to look their best. All of them being, wives of senior Profs, were quite matronly weighing in the range of seventy five to eighty five kg. The heaviest lady, the wife of the Dean of Students, was made the anchor. Another heavy lady was the wife of the Prof who was the honorary chairman of sports. This fact was later to become a source of difficulty for Mr. Nand Kumar.

There could not have been a greater contrast between the two teams. Many students compared it to a contest of bulldozers against racing cars. To the audience it seemed that the ladies would simply pull the girls over with just a gentle flick of their wrists. Many bets were made on the time it would take for the ladies to pull the girls.

Only Vinod felt that the girls would win. He did not merely feel that way, but was quite confident of the outcome. He reasoned that the girls though slim had strong muscles while the ladies were overweight and were all fat and no muscles. They all had servants and maids to do their house work and so their muscles had not been used for years. Also the skin of their palms and fingers was so soft and tender that griping and pulling the rough rope would cause them pain.

Many of his class mates bet against him on high odds of five to one or even higher. Vinod was quietly confident of winning a huge sum of money while those betting against him were equally sure of winning. A few other discerning members of the audience also realized these facts but felt that it would be a close contest and they reasoned that the result would be the same as in case of the men's event. Vinod reasoned that the boys did not want to displease the senior Profs as they held the power to award marks. The girls had no such reason to be afraid of the ladies. For them it was a straightforward case of trying their best to win.

The two teams were lined up holding the rope tightly while the audience watched with bated breath as Mr. Kumar blew the whistle. The contest was over almost before it started. No, the ladies did not win. At the very first pull by the girls, the first three ladies fell forward on their faces. The rest let go of the rope which stung their hands. The entire force was now transferred to the anchor lady. The rope tightened around her waist like a python. She toppled forward and was dragged along the ground for several feet. The spectacle created quite a bit of mirth among the audience. Some of the coarser elements burst into loud howls of hyena like laughter.

After this performance it was understandable that the ladies were reluctant for the second round. However, Mr. Kumar and his band of assistants used all of their powers of persuasion to get them lined up for the next attempt. He told them that the first pull was a fluke result and that they were probably not ready when the whistle was blown and so the girls took them by surprise. He advised them to lean backwards and dig their heels into the ground and let the girls tire themselves. After this they could easily pull the girls over. Mr. Kumar asserted that he was sure of their victory.

Although the ladies tried their best to follow his advice, his assertion of victory was proved to be totally false. This time also the result was the same but the manner of losing was totally different. At the start the ladies promptly leaned back and tried to dig their heels in to let the girls do the pulling. For some time they held their ground but then were pulled forward a little bit. Then they leaned back even more and this proved to be their undoing. Most of them lost balance and were about to fall. Mr. Kumar had explained to them that a team loses the contest if its members hold the rope while their bodies are in contact with the ground.

Using great presence of mind they all let go of the rope. This time the anchor lady was extremely alert. In the first contest her stomach had been squeezed by the rope and she had also been dragged along the ground. It had hurt her physically and also wounded her pride when the students laughed at her. As soon as she saw what was about to happen, she uncoiled the rope from around her waist and shoulder and let it go. Miraculously the timing of all of the ladies was near perfect. They all released the rope almost simultaneously. Meanwhile the girls had been intent on tugging the rope hard. As soon as the rope became free, the lead girls staggered backwards and all of them fell in one great big heap.

The combined spectacle of the ladies falling flat on their bottoms and the girls falling on top of each other was too much for the audience. This time the laughter was much louder and lasted much longer. Even some of the strict Profs, who had never been seen to smile, burst into loud laughter. Of course none of husbands laughed, partly because of concern for their wives and largely to avoid unpleasantness at the home front.

The other consequences of the contest were both good as well as bad. It was bad for Mr. Kumar. The ladies held him responsible for their humiliation. After all the ladies tug of war was his brain child. Later that year the interview for his confirmation as head coach was held. The ladies prevailed upon their husbands to reject his confirmation. Fortunately for him he got his confirmation two years later, because as the saying goes, a good man cannot be kept down.

A good consequence was that the ladies had become such objects of ridicule, that their husbands could persuade them to lose weight and improve their physical fitness. The sports organization arranged for early morning yoga and physical fitness classes for the ladies, which most of them started attending.

For most of the students that tug of war remained the funniest event of their college days. The story was told and retold many times and was passed over to future batches of students. For Vinod it was an especially memorable day because he had pocketed a princely sum of money from his two bets. The ladies tug of war brought him much more. When his friends asked him what was the source of his inside info on the men's tug of war. He replied that Mr. Kumar was his father's childhood friend and had told him about the tradition and asserted that it would be followed. Later, it was Mr. Kumar who told him about his failure to be confirmed in his job that year and his success two years later.

While these four friends were recalling the ladies tug of war, it is quite likely that several others were also recalling the same event.

****

An Old Man Decides

They were driving from Delhi to Nahan, a small hill town in Himachal Pradesh. The old man sat in front with his son who was driving. His sister, daughter in law and little grandson sat at the back. They were visiting his uncle and family to spend a week with them. The guests and hosts were eagerly looking forward to this long due visit. The drive through Delhi had been tedious but driving on the highway through the Haryana countryside was pleasant.

At around noon they stopped at a wayside complex which had a number of eateries, shops and factory outlets. Some friend had recommended a particular dhaba which was famous for its stuffed parathas served with large pats of butter, pickles, and curd.

The meal tickled everyone's palate and they talked excitedly while eating, but the old man was silent. He ate absentmindedly while his thoughts drifted back by seventy years to his childhood days. Nahan had always been his favorite town. It was his mother's home town. Her parents, brothers and their families and many other relations lived there.

During his childhood days the journey would start at Agra, where he lived with his parents and younger sister. Every summer they had vacations from the first week of May till the second week of July and they would invariably spend most of this period at Nahan. He always thought of the summer days as the best days of the year- no school and the special charm of a couple of months spent with close relations in the pleasant climate of the hills of Nahan and plenty of kite flying, which he loved. A visit to the home of every relation in Nahan was a must. Any relation omitted, would feel hurt.

The family would board the train at Agra with their luggage, which consisted of steel trunks for clothes and holdalls for beddings. Drinking water had to be carried in an earthen pitcher named surai, which was housed in a protective wooden bracket. They would break journey at New Delhi to spend four or five days with his father's relations and another couple of days with his mother's cousin, who was the manager of a hotel in old Delhi. At the former his time was spent in playing with his cousins and reading books, while at the hotel the main charm was flying kites all day long from the hotel roof.

The next leg of the journey was by train to Ambala and further by bus to Kala Amb, a little town where the plains ended and the hills began, and then another bus to Nahan. The buses were smaller and less comfortable as they did not have seats like today, but had four long parallel wooden benches along the length of the bus and another at the back across the width. There were no eating places on the way, so food and water had to be carried. Despite this the old man felt the journey in the old days was more enjoyable. His thoughts came to an abrupt end as everyone had finished and were ready to visit the shops and factory outlets before resuming the journey.

Soon they could see the hills and crossed the bridge on the river Narkanda, a short distance before Kala Amb. Earlier there was no bridge and the bus crossed through the river which did not have much water in May, but in July it could be a different matter. There was more water and there was the possibility of flash floods which could topple the bus and drown the passengers. The bridge had made the crossing a simple matter but he missed the excitement of crossing through the river.

Kala Amb onwards the road was a narrow, winding hill road with hairpin bends and steep ascents. If a bus came from the opposite direction then one of them would have to wait where the road was wider till the other bus crossed it. Now the road had been widened and two buses could cross each other with ease.

In the old days there was a check point where the bus halted and the passengers were inoculated. This was done to prevent the spread of some epidemic disease from the plains to the hills. Probably it was cholera and the injection was quite painful, but now this was no longer needed.

Soon they could see the former ruler's palace and a couple of other large buildings while they were still a few miles short of Nahan. Most of the houses in the old days were single storied with the roofs constructed of parallel wooden girders with slate squares on them and a top layer of red clay. This provided good insulation in summer as well as winter. The clay surface had a good slope to drain rain water and there was no leakage. During rains, the water flowing from the roofs acquired a striking reddish, pink color due to some clay being washed away. After a few years people would lay more clay on the roof.

The town was small and there had been open spaces between the houses with trees and gardens. The population had grown manifold. Most of the open spaces and gardens had been replaced by houses which were mainly three or four storied and made of brick and concrete. The town had become extremely congested. It was difficult to drive through the streets because of the cars and motor cycles parked on both sides of the road. Finally they did manage to find parking on the roof of a building with the help of his uncle and cousin who were waiting for them. The roof was at road level and the parking charges were quite high. About a dozen other cars were parked there

That night they sat together talking till long past midnight. His sister and son had visited the town earlier and were disappointed to see its changed condition. The daughter in law and grandson were impressed because it was their first visit and they looked forward to meeting many relations for the first time. The next few days were spent in visiting relations and walking around the town to see the quaint old markets and the temples. One day they drove many kilometers to visit the Renuka Lake for boating and to visit its temples. The place was surrounded by hills which added to its natural beauty.

As usual, the old man could not sleep well that night. His thoughts turned to his late wife. She had passed away recently after a serious illness which had lasted several years. Her suffering and passing away had a profound effect on him and would haunt him as long as he lived. She had been a source of great moral support to him and her mere presence calmed his nerves when he was in difficulty. Now her absence made him feel lonely and helpless.

He was worried about his future. Too many of his relations had suffered before they died. His grandmother, father, mother in law and brother in law had all battled against cancer before succumbing. He lamented, "Oh why does god cause pain and suffering to honest and noble souls?"

He was not afraid of dying but did not want to suffer and die like them. He thought, if only he could go to sleep and never wake up, that would be the best way of getting relieved from his worldly problems. Unfortunately one can't choose one's manner of passing away.

His thoughts drifted back to the Nahan of today. The town had changed for the worse. It had become congested and the trees and birds were all gone. Children did not fly kites any more. The maximum time to walk from one end of the town to the other end was forty or fifty minutes at the most. Yet people sped around in cars and motorcycles. Even in the narrow lanes he saw motorcycles speeding, and shoppers dodging out of the way. What was the urgent hurry? Were these people mad? If they had walked, it would have taken only a few minutes more.

He felt the town had lost much of its charm. From being his favorite place it had become forbidding and uncaring. What about the other cities? Agra and Delhi had also changed. Their souls had been crushed by progress. From being pleasant cities with good living conditions and friendly people they had become huge overcrowded monstrosities with equally monstrous problems of traffic and pollution. The people were less friendly and caring. They were cold and heartless. A man could get injured in a street accident or a lady could be robbed in broad daylight and no one would come to their aid.

The same could be said about the world. His childhood had been a time of hope and joy. Hope for a bright future based on progress and scientific development. When young he thought that most diseases would be eliminated and poverty would become non-existent. Nuclear energy would generate enough power to satisfy the needs of humankind. The UN would work as an agency which would bring about peace and harmony. This was also the feeling of most other people in those times.

It was true that there had been progress in many fields. Computers, electronics and IT had revolutionized the world. Food production had increased by leaps and bounds. Many epidemic diseases had been eliminated or brought under control, but then some new diseases had cropped up as if from nowhere. Other diseases had developed drug resistance. Further, most drugs had dangerous side effects. The medical profession had become highly commercialized.

Poverty was eliminated in some countries, but in others the situation had become worse. What about the rag pickers and the farmers committing suicide due to debt and poverty? The vast increase in population was reducing the habitats of wildlife and bringing many species to the verge of extinction. The use of pesticides and other harmful chemicals used to grow farm produce, to fatten animals and to increase milk yield, was playing further havoc with the environment. The oceans were being polluted by harmful chemicals, plastics and polythene.

Could marine life survive under such conditions? Governments were callously spending huge amounts on arms and weapons of mass destruction. This money could very well have been spent on controlling pollution and on human welfare.

Another big problem was the rise of fanatics and terrorists and conflicts between nations. The efforts of the UN or mediators could not resolve these issues. Moreover the danger of nuclear weapons falling into the hands of terrorists was increasing.

On the other hand, many countries had achieved high standards of living, and health. Some knowledgeable scientist had calculated that if the rest of the world were to achieve the same standards, then it would require the resources of four planets the size of our earth. Could development and human ingenuity find the resources? A few years ago the old man would have replied in the affirmative but today he was not sure.

The biggest problem of all was of global warming. Many nations recognized it as the greatest challenge facing the world but some denied it and others were least concerned about it. Melting of polar ice would raise sea levels, which would submerge vast habitable areas. The temperature rise would make life difficult if not impossible for people, animals and plants. Was the human race hurtling to its doom at an ever increasing pace? The end would certainly not come during his life time, but what about the fate of his children, grandchildren and their descendants and those of his friends and relations? His heart ached at the thought.

Many times he had thought deeply about these matters. What had gone wrong since his childhood days to create the present situation? Was it the fault of the leaders or the people? Could the world have developed in a different manner since his childhood? Could not some wise and sensible leaders have guided human destiny in a more humane manner towards sustainable development?

These questions had no firm answers. Better minds than his had deliberated on such issues without arriving at satisfactory answers. He felt that there was no connection between industrial growth and wisdom. Though knowledge and the capacity to cause harm had grown astronomically since his childhood, yet there had been no increase in wisdom. He felt that the collective wisdom of the human race had reached its lowest level ever.

In his opinion, the world had two choices. The first was to halt industrial growth and concentrate on conservation. The other was rapid scientific development and progress which, he felt, might lead to disaster or to salvation. His mind could not decide as it was old and tired and was in need of rest. It had governed his actions for far too long. Was it not time for the heart to take over, to decide in favor of days long gone by, when hope and joy ruled supreme? The tussle between heart and mind lasted for what seemed to him like an eternity. His mind was that of an old man while the heart was that of a child. Finally the child prevailed and he remembered a favorite song from his childhood: Que Sara Sara, whatever will be, will be. The future's not ours to see.

He decided this was the truth, which would let him live his life at peace with the world and he would let the world move forward in its own mysterious way. That night was the first night when he slept soundly after many years. Next morning he awoke refreshed and cheerful. Having made his decision he felt relieved of a heavy burden. From now on he would be happy and cheerful for the sake of his near and dear ones and leave the fate of the world in the hands of the younger generation.

****

The Absent Minded Professor

There is a wide spread impression in the minds of the public that all Profs are absentminded. Nothing can be further from the truth. The vast majority of Profs are basically quite normal,

intelligent, beings. However there are some who are absent minded. This variety, though small in numbers, adds flavor to the Professorial reputation, in the same way as salt and spices add flavor to a dish.

SBY was one such absent minded Prof and was regarded by most students to be an eccentric as well. He was a bachelor in his early thirties and was an Associate Prof, but it is common to refer to all university teachers as Prof. The students used to tell many tales about him.

One was about the time a night watchman found his office door open and papers strewn all over the place. Naturally, he thought that a burglary had taken place. He and the other guards rushed to the Bachelor Hostel and found the Prof's door was open. They rushed into the room and found that SBY was sleeping on the ground in a corner while his walking stick was lying on the bed. The guards woke him up. He muttered, "After returning from my walk, I must have put my stick on the bed by mistake and parked myself in the corner."

The guards said, "Pease come with us to your office. A robbery has occurred there."

They all rushed to his office. SBY walked in and took a quick look around and announced, "There has been no robbery. Everything is exactly as I left it. It's just that I forgot to shut the door. By the time I come to office tomorrow, the room will be in a neat and tidy condition. I have a research scholar who tidies my office every morning."

The guards left feeling that it was a case of, 'Much ado about nothing'.

The research scholar referred to was a girl named RMX. She was in her early twenties and average in looks but much above average in intelligence and commonsense, which is a rare quality in researchers. After all, they do not research for the common but for the unusual and the new. He was not her first choice as a guide, but had been appointed because he had the least number of scholars under his guidance.

At first she was disappointed, but then decided to make the best of a bad bargain. Soon she viewed him as a matrimonial prospect and thought of him as a rough cut diamond which would need much more polishing than the hardest of rough cut diamonds. Once her topic of research was decided, she settled down in her task of research as well as diamond polishing. It is easy to say that the diamond polishing task was far more difficult, because the diamond offered much resistance and argued against every suggestion for improvement.

The morning after the so called robbery, she reached the office and removed the clutter by sorting all papers and putting everything back in its right place. Like most women, she was highly allergic to clutter and could not concentrate on her research in its midst. He on the other hand (like many men) did not feel comfortable unless surrounded by clutter. He differed from her as much as chalk from cheese.

That morning he strolled into the office blissfully unaware that one of his socks was bright red and the other an equally bright green. Her keen eyes immediately detected this abominable mistake because of the huge gap between the shoe tops and the trouser legs.

She said, "Sir, your socks are of two different colors. You must return home and change one of them to match the other."

SBY looked down and seeing the contrasting colors replied, "It is not my fault. The manufacturer has not ensured good quality control. I have another pair in which one is red and the other is green."

RMX replied firmly, "Kindly don't transfer the blame on to the manufacturer. Please go home immediately and take off the red sock and put on a green one instead."

SBY objected, "But then I will be mixing up socks from two different pairs."

RMX suppressed her irritation and spoke as politely as possible, "Sir, can't you understand that the manufacturer has made no mistake. It is you who has mixed up a red pair with a green pair?"

SBY did not quite agree with her but had learned from experience that her opinion would prevail. He replied weakly, "You may be right, but why should I waste time in going back just to change the socks. I can do that when I go back at lunch time."

RMX responded, "Sir, you have a lecture of the third year B Tech class and they will laugh and make jokes about your socks."

SBY responded, "They are always quiet in my class. I don't bother if they chatter and laugh outside the class."

RMX responded, "The story of your socks will be conveyed to all research scholars. They will make jokes about you in the scholar's common room. That will embarrass me."

SBY, "It does not embarrass me, so why does it bother you."

RMX, "You are my guide. Anything which ridicules you upsets me and I cannot concentrate on my research work when I am upset."

SBY did not have any reply for this, so he reluctantly trudged back to his hostel room to change the socks."

They had been arguing ever since he had become her guide. At first the arguments pertained mainly to her research topic and its scope. At some stage she had made it clear to him that she needed no further guidance and would complete the rest of the works without his help or advice. He told her that if the thesis is rejected she should not blame him. Her confident reply was that she knew what she was doing and there was no possibility of rejection. From that day onwards their roles had been reversed. She had started guiding him in all matters concerning his clothes, appearance and behavior. It was part of her role as a diamond polisher.

Though nothing was said between them, yet at some stage he had understood that as soon as she completed her thesis, she intended to marry him. He accepted this fate because he had become dependent on her guidance. She was determined to marry him because she had invested so much time and effort in polishing him- why let a polished diamond fall into the hands of another woman.

These reasons might not seem to be romantic, but they were basically sound reasons. It was a subdued love story which was vastly different from those depicted on the film screen or in romantic novels. After all academicians don't behave like film stars.

In due course of time she submitted her thesis. It was approved by the external examiners who praised its high quality. The viva was also a grand success. Her presentation was excellent and she gave logical answers to all questions raised by the examiner and members of the audience.

The senior faculty members were so impressed that they advised her to apply for the position of Assistant Prof. Now she had the degree and also a job was assured.

Soon they got married. By now SBY had become less absentminded and had developed into a far more confident and smart person. In other words he had become as much of a polished diamond as was possible.

The day after their marriage he said to her, "You are the most beautiful woman in the whole world."

She blushed coyly but did not contradict him. Then he added, "And I am the most intelligent Prof in the whole world."

This time she contradicted him and he gave a fitting reply, "If I am not the most intelligent Prof, then please explain how I managed to marry the most beautiful woman in the whole world."

She had no answer. She had lost an argument to him for the first time. This was the auspicious start of their long and happy married life.

****

An Accounts Officer Finds Gold

It was hot! The afternoon sun rays beat down oppressively on Murari Lal. We are far removed in time and so can take the liberty of dropping the prefix Mr. from his name- a liberty which all except his superiors took at their own risk. After all he was an assistant accounts officer with thirty years of experience of which two thirds had been under British rule. The fact that he was only a matriculate did not lower his self esteem one bit. On numerous occasions he had told his younger colleagues, "The Matric pass of our time is any day superior to the MA of today".

If the office peon did not address him respectfully, then sure as hell, he was in for at least a week, if not a month, of extra work and scolding. It was much worse if one of the many members of the general public, submitting a loan application, did so. Murari Lal would color the application red with objections, with the result that the Senior Accounts Officer would have no choice but to reject it.

Anyway we have deviated far from the present scene, in which Murari was lost in the desert in Rajasthan. Actually he was only a short distance away from the ancient fortress of Lakshman Garh close to the present day town of Bhawanipur. If he had but walked fifty steps to the top of the small hill on his east, he would have clearly seen the right lockout tower of the fort scarcely half a kilometer or so away.

It is no real mystery why he did not climb up the hill, but to understand that you have to know all of the facts. Fact number one is that no accounts rule in the world says that to see further away you must climb a hill. Of course Murari knew that one can see a greater distance from a height but that, in his opinion, was just an abstract fact having no bearing in this particular case. After all each case is different and so is every hill. What was the guarantee that he could see the fort from the top of the hill? So why waste precious energy on climbing a hill when one can walk on level ground or better still go down a slope into a ravine.

Now this one fact is enough because no sensible accounts man raises all of his objections in one go. That is the first and most important lesson one learns. So that is the path he took. He entered into the nearest ravine. He imagined he had a long search ahead of him and what better way to save energy than to walk down a slope. After all an ounce of energy saved is an ounce of energy earned. No matter that the saying is for a penny, but when you are lost in the desert then a penny or for that matter a rupee or a pound or even a dollar are all worthless and energy reigns supreme. This is particularly more so if you are also feeling weak from thirst and exhaustion.

We have again deviated from the story. Naturally the reader would be curious to know about what brought Murari to Rajasthan and the circumstances under which he came to be lost? The answer to the first part is really quite simple. He had come with a group from his office to audit the accounts of the Lakshman Garh Fort which had a large income from the sale of entry tickets and an even larger expenditure on its repair and maintenance. It was the latter about which the Rajasthan government had its suspicions and which it wanted checked by an external audit party from Delhi. The chief accounts officer, Bhagwan Das himself was a most upright and honest man and he had selected Murari Lal as his lieutenant and trusted right hand man in the team.

There were two others in the team, Chalia Mul and Kapti Das, whom as their names suggested, he could not trust completely and counted upon Murari to ensure that the audit was honest and above board. This Murari did quite well. It was three days since their arrival and he had already found several major errors in the expenses which Messers Chalia and Kapti had overlooked. In some items the expenses were so highly inflated which only the blind or the completely ignorant could have failed to see. All of this made him suspect that the two were taking bribes to turn a blind eye to corruption.

The fourth day being a Sunday, they went to visit a famous old temple a good three kilometers from the town. The road was not motorable, being just a narrow path which skirted the ravines, but it was said that a visit to the Temple brought good luck to the true devotee. The partyconsisted of Murari, Chalia and Kapti and the two peons, Bhana Mal and Ralia Ram who were carrying the packed lunch and water.

They left their dak bungalow after breakfast and reached the temple in good time. It was while returning that Chalia suggested that they take a short cut which would save them a kilometer and a half. He said that the temple priest had told him about it. Being tired Murari readily agreed.

This short cut led them through the ravines and some low rolling hills. Being older and heavier than the others Murari lagged behind and at some point lost his way. His getting lost was possibly as simple as that, but was it really so? However, Murari had an altogether different explanation. He thought it was a diabolical plot hatched by that crook Chalia and his co-conspirator Kapti in league with the two peons to get rid of him. Hadn't he heard countless stories about people getting lost in the deserts of Rajasthan and dying of the heat and thirst?

Only a few weeks ago he had seen a film in which the same thing happened to the villain. This was the cleverest way to murder him and not be blamed for it. At worst they would get a reprimand for losing him in the desert. With these depressing thoughts in mind, he struggled along, through one ravine after the other, getter hotter and more tired by the minute. What about the gold? We believe there was some mention of gold in the story or was it maybe in the title? The reader may be impatient for the gold to turn up but he will have to wait a bit.

That is exactly what Murari did. Tired and short of breath he decided to wait awhile and sat down on a large red colored boulder to rest. He just did not know how to get out of this maze of ravines. He cursed Chalia and Kapti repeatedly but then saw that it was an exercise in futility. Getting into a state of hopelessness, he prayed to god that if he ever got back safely he would never meddle in the affairs of others. He had learnt his lesson well and truly and would never come in the way of Chalia and Kapti and their wrongdoing.

In his frustration he picked up a stone and threw it against the opposite slope where, to his amazement, it started a mini landslide. Loose earth, some pebbles and a few boulders rolled down and formed a heap almost at his feet. The accompanying cloud of dust covered him from head to foot. On dusting himself, he spotted a shiny yellow colored, metallic object in the heap, which he picked up with considerable effort. It was heavy, irregularly shaped having several small protrusions and some stubby branches. It appeared to be either an extremely irregular piece of naturally occurring gold or a hidden collection of gold jewelry, melted into this shape by a chance bolt of lightning, or maybe some jewelry crudely melted by some thieves and hidden in some bygone era. He judged it to weigh at least ten kilos if not more.

"Gold!" He exclaimed, his mood changing from utter despondency to supreme euphoria, "I have found real gold. I am rich!"

He was due to retire the next year. Visions of a luxurious retired life floated in front of him. He would dispose his faithful old motorbike and buy a brand new Fiat. His wife would be happy to get some new furniture and saris and they would be able to afford a servant and summer visits to some hill stations like Shimla, Nainital or Mussoorie. His sons would get some share in the wealth. He was in the seventh heaven of delight.

Reality soon brought him down to earth. There still remained the problem of finding his way back and that too while carrying the heavy gold. Also there were other problems. Even if he managed to get back with the gold he could not hide it from prying eyes. Chalia and Kapti would be most suspicious. He would have to disclose the gold. He reasoned that if it was a long lost treasure then it belonged to the state and he could not keep it. If it was stolen property then he might be accused of stealing and melting it. If it was naturally occurring gold then he would have to surrender it to the government as he did not have the mining rights.

"Why should the government get something for doing nothing? It is just not fair. After all it is my life which is at risk and I have always served the government honestly and faithfully all my life. So why I am not entitled to keep this gold?" Murari grumbled to himself and dropped the idea of carrying it back with him.

He thought about the possibility of hiding it and coming back to collect it at some future date. He would bring his sons with him and also tools to cut it into small pieces which could be easily concealed and carried. They would sell it to the goldsmith whom he and his wife had patronized for the last twenty five years or so. The man knew him well and was a reasonable person. Of course he would wonder how a service class man like Murari suddenly got so much gold and in such odd pieces.

"Would it not be better to sell it to different jewelers in different places?" thought Murari. "No this will increase the risk of someone informing the police or the tax people", his better sense told him. His regular goldsmith appeared to be the safest bet. The man was discreet. He would probably offer him about ten percent less than the market price but then it was only fair for him to make a profit in this type of deal.

What about his lavish post retirement life style? Wouldn't people wonder about it? It would surely be the talk of his office. Chalia and Kapti would tell one and all "Look at his life style. Can a pensioner afford to live like this? Surely he was even more corrupt than us even while posing to be such an honest and rule abiding person."

"Let Chalia and Kapti spew as much venom as they like, but they have no real proof about any wrong doing. So, it is I, Mr. Murari Lal, who will have the last laugh." muttered Murari to himself with satisfaction.

He sat down on a boulder and took stock of the risks, expenses and profits. There was some element of risk, also some effort and discomfort had gone in as the capital, and the expenditure was only ten percent commission, which the goldsmith would charge, while the profit was ninety percent.

Any company would be superlatively happy with such a balance sheet, but not Murari. Unearned wealth went against his principles. True he had walked around in the scorching sun, but that effort was directed in saving his own life and not looking for the gold. He had come across it purely by accident. He had not earned it through his hard labor. More importantly it was utterly dishonest to keep the gold as he would be breaking many rules. He could neither disclose the gold as his income nor pay tax on it. It would simply be ill gotten wealth which never does anyone any good. By keeping it he would be lowering himself to the level of Chalia and Kapti.

It was true that he had been sorely tempted to keep the wealth, but then he was only human and there was still time to act according to the dictates of his conscience. He really did not need the wealth and luxury that goes with it. He and his wife could manage on his pension and his sons were self sufficient, being gainfully employed. He firmly resolved to bury the gold and not recover it later.

The readers may or may not approve of his reasoning and decision; but then every individual has a different background and principles. Using a pointed stone Murari scooped out a hole in the ground deep enough to bury the gold and cover it with a foot thick layer of soil. Over this he placed the debris brought down by the stone he had thrown earlier.

In two or three hours at most the sun would set and gradually it would become dark. For a fleeting moment he imagined all kinds of wild beasts searching for their prey at night, with no tree in sight which he could climb and spend the night safe from their attack.

Soon his moment of fear passed and he was his rational self again. He remembered that the temple was due west from the fort so he must travel east. He walked through the ravines so that the afternoon sun was on his back. In this way he managed to reach the gate of the fort well before sunset. There he rested a while and refreshed himself at the tea shop before proceeding to the dak bungalow.

This is most certainly not the happy end of the story. Murari was firm in hisdecision and was never tempted to return to Bhawanipur and search for the gold. He didnot even mention it to his wife or children or even his most trusted friends. So the secret went with him to the grave. For all you know the gold is still where he buried it. The possibility of another traveler getting lost and going to the same ravine is pretty slim. Further the probability that he would dig at the same spot for no reason at all maybe less even than one in a trillion.

The gold is most certainly waiting for the alert reader to find it. You simply have to work backwards on the route that he took from the ravine to the gate of the fort and find the red colored boulder. It will be helpful if you pack a spade, some cutting tools, a bag and a metal detector before launching on this endeavor. The story will have a happy ending when you find the gold.

****

Tales and Trivia from Academia III

The Missing `x': A senior Prof of Maths was due to retire. He had been teaching a particular subject for the past many years. This was allotted to another Prof GNX, who had never taught that subject before. So he requested him for his lecture notes. The well prepared notes made his task easier. One day he was writing some formulae on the board.

A student raised a question, "Sir what happened to the `x' on the left hand side of the equation. It is not there on the right hand side."

Prof GNX looked at the equation and saw that the `x' was there on the left hand side but not on the right hand side. This puzzled him and he consulted the notes but they also did not have an 'x' on the right hand side. The other students were also puzzled and all tried to check the formulae for any mistakes. Then GNX and the entire class spent around forty five minutes puzzling over the missing 'x'.

Finally one student came up with an explanation. He said, "I think it is a multiplication sign and not 'x'. That is why it has disappeared after the multiplication was done. Thus the mystery was solved.

Prof GNX thanked him, took out his red pen, circled the 'x' in his notes, and wrote 'multiplication sign and not x', so that there would be no confusion in the future.

The Tea War: The Boston tea party had great and long lasting consequences for the entire world. It led to the American war of Independence. After much fighting and many deaths USA gained independence from Great Britain. Today it is the most powerful country in the whole world. The tea war of this story, though fought on a much smaller scale and in a peaceful manner, was fought equally seriously by the two parties.

Mathematics is an abstract subject. To conduct research in Mathematics a person must have a high IQ and a high capacity for concentration. A group of Profs found that drinking frequent cups of tea was conducive for research. They would spend a lot of time discussing research ideas over cups of tea in their department. When they visited each other's homes, there also, they would start discussing their research with each other while sipping cups of tea served by the ladies.

The latter were thoroughly bored by having to listen to research discussions. Finally Mrs. VKX took matters into her hands. She called the ladies to her home and said, "I am sick and tired listening to their boring Maths talk. What should we do?"

They all agreed that they were also fed up listening to the Mathematical chatter which made no sense to them.

One said, "Our husbands spend most of their time in the department drinking tea and only pretend to do great research. None of them has won any big award."

Another one added, "Drinking so many cups of tea with sugar is an invitation to diabetes."

Mrs. VKX said, "Let us decide that no more tea will be served at home during social visits. Instead we will serve nimbupani with salt and jeera. If they talk about Maths we must talk loudly about movies or shopping to drown out their conversation. Also, we must convince our husbands to drink tea without sugar in the office. Make them see that it is for their own good."

From that day onwards Mrs. VKX's decisions were implemented rigorously. At first there was opposition from most of the husbands. After all, very few men would allow their privileges to be taken away easily. They argued that they were not drinking liquor but tea which helped them in concentrating on research. The ladies did not buy this argument and stoutly stood their ground.

A few husbands were willing to make a compromise. However, Prof RDX was very upset by this turn of events. He had a strong dislike for nimbupani with jeera, and resented the ban on Maths discussions. He was determined to have his revenge on the ladies.

After a few weeks, most of the ladies went shopping in the main market in the town, which was at a considerable distance from their campus. There was a sudden strike call by the transporters union and all taxis, scooters, rickshaws and buses stopped plying. Prof RDX heard the news on the radio and he sensed an opportunity to get his revenge.

He hopped into the car and drove towards the town. He had guessed that he would find the ladies stranded at the main bus stand, waiting in vain for a bus or any other means of transport. His guess was right. As soon as the ladies saw his car they were delighted and rushed towards it. He firmly refused to open the door unless they apologized and agreed to serve tea at home and not interrupt the discussions on Maths.

The ladies protested loudly and accused him of blackmail. There was much argumentation and hard bargaining for terms and conditions. Prof RDX agreed to drive back with his wife and inform the other husbands so that they would drive over and pick up the other ladies. The matter of serving tea and the Maths discussions would be sorted out later in a meeting at which all husbands and wives would be present.

Eventually the matter was resolved after much hard bargaining and argument. Tea without sugar would be served at home by the host lady and Maths discussions would be allowed only if no other ladies were present. If any other lady was present then nimbupani would be served and it was forbidden to discuss Maths. As for tea in the office, the husbands agreed to restrict themselves to a maximum of three small cups- some of them agreed to take it without sugar.

This fortunate outcome was in sharp contrast to the matter of the Boston tea party which resulted in the American war of independence. By the way, the story was narrated to me by Prof RDX. I cannot vouch for its veracity since he was known for enhancing his role in all matters.

The PhD examination: One day before the vivo-voce, the examiner Prof SQY arrived by the evening train. The PhD scholar MRX and his guide Prof PNY received him at the station and escorted him to the college guest house. They left after ensuring that he was comfortably settled in his room.

The next day the exam started punctually at 10 AM in the department meeting hall. Several Profs and scholars were present. MRX made his presentation with the help of a slide projector. The topic was rather obscure and most of the Profs and Scholars had only a vague knowledge of and interest in it. Even then they tried their best to understand the presentation but failed to do so and soon last interest.

After the presentation, SQY asked many questions and MRX responded. Sometimes PNY would also join in. Soon it developed into a tripartite discussion involving SQY, MRX and PNY. The others could hardly make out head or tale of it, but could feel the enthusiasm and keen interest of the three.

Soon it was time for the lunch hosted by MRX. Most persons ate the lunch heartily but the three protagonists kept up a lively discussion on the topic. Their interest in the topic was so keen that they barely ate any of the delicious items.

After lunch, the guests dispersed and the three protagonists proceeded to the guest house where their discussion continued even while SQY packed his belongings and also during the taxi ride to the station. On alighting they proceeded to the platform and resumed their discussion with lively vigor.

The train arrived but the three remained blissfully unaware. Finally when the guard blew the whistle and the train started moving, the three suddenly realized what had happed. They made a mad dash to board the train. Finally when the train went clear of the platform MRX and PNY had boarded the train with the luggage of SQY. They would have to get down at the next stop and return. The worst part was that SQY, being older and heavier, could not run so fast and was left behind. He consoled himself by thinking that he would get another day to discuss the topic with MRX and PNY.

VOID RATIO: This is an important term encountered in the subject of Soil Mechanics, a subject which is useful for design of foundations of any structure. Void ratio is defined as the volume of voids or empty space in a unit volume of soil. Prof GRY had taught this subject many times during his career and was an expert in foundations.

Once he visited a construction site to give technical advice. The Executive Engineer (EE) at the site greeted him and introduced himself, “Sir, you may not recognize me, but many years ago I was a student at your institute and you had taught one subject to our class.”

GRY responded, "Glad to meet an old student of mine after so many years. What was the name of the subject?”

The EE responded, “I am sorry Sir, but I do not remember the name of the subject. I only remember you taught us about something which was known as Void Ratio.

GRY was taken aback. His ego was hurt that the student did not even remember the name of the subject. Then he realized that he did not even remember the student even after meeting him. His ignorance more than evened out the student’s ignorance.

This little incident illustrates a big truth. Our Universities and IITs are vast store houses of knowledge because the students leave much of their knowledge behind at the time of graduating. This leads us to the next joke.

The Convocation: The Director reached the podium to start his farewell speech to the graduating students. He picked up the typed speech and was about to start reading it. One student shouted, “Sir, we are fed up of listening to long and boring lectures for the past four years. Just tell us a short joke instead of your prepared speech.”

The Director put down the papers and said, “Ok! I hope you like the joke. You all know quite well that our institute is regarded as the biggest store house of knowledge in the country. Now, I will tell you the secret behind how we accumulated so much knowledge. Each batch of students spends four years struggling to acquire knowledge. At the time of graduating they donate all of it to the institute in exchange for their degrees. My sincere advice to you it is to try to retain some of it because it will come in handy in your professional career.”

This short, sarcastic speech was far more effective than any long lecture would have been. It made the students realize the true value of the knowledge they had gained.

****

The Trophy Hunter

John was sitting on a machan about seven or eight meters above the ground waiting for the arrival of the tiger. The machan had been erected that very morning and John had been there since then and it was now past noon. Between the machan and the forest edge there was a pond about fifteen to twenty meters in diameter. If the tiger emerged from the forest and drank from the far side of the pond, the distance from John would be around seventy meters. At this distance it would be an easy shot using his rifle, which had a telescopic sight.

He had been born in the 1890ies to Anglo-India parents in British India and was now in his mid thirties. He was a successful businessman who quarried limestone from the hills near Dehradoon and supplied it to industries in Delhi making big profits each year. He and his wife Alice lived in a large inherited colonial style house which had been constructed by John's grandparents in the outskirts of Dehradoon. Their two children studied in a boarding school in Mussoorie and come home during vacations and on occasional weekends when permitted by the Principal.

The house had large old style rooms and was on a large ground with many old leechi trees, lawns and flower beds. These were maintained by the mali, who lived in one of the servant quarters at the back of the ground. Alice was particularly fond of flowers and guided the mali to maintain their garden, in such good shape, that it was one of the finest in Dehradoon.

John was an avid trophy hunter. Over the years he had shot many animals and birds. Heads and skins of a leopard, a bear and several varieties of deer were mounted on the drawing room walls. In one corner was a large glass cabinet with a large number of stuffed birds of many kinds. He had given away several leopard, bear, dear and other animal heads and skins to his friends. Between the leopard and the bear was a large space reserved for a tiger head and its skin, which he had failed to shoot till now. This failure had caused him much agony.

Alice did not approve of this display of animal and bird trophies in their home. She considered it to be vulgar and repeatedly said that she would prefer to put up paintings and fresh flowers from their garden. She did not object to hunting for meat but was against wanton killing of animals for the sake of trophies.

Many times she would say, "Oh John, I wish you would not kill so many animals simply for your trophies. You know that Jim Corbett kills only the man eating leopards and tigers. The only other animals and birds he kills are for his food or to give away to poor people. I wish you would copy his example." Her words had no effect on him.

Once or twice a month they would invite Anglo-Indian and Indian friends for dinner. These were lavish affairs. After dinner the ladies would move to a side room to drink sherbet or grape wine, while the men moved into the drawing room for hard liquor.

After the first sip, John would tell his hunting tales. He had a vast collection in his repertoire and was an excellent story teller. The men would listen to him with rapt attention. Some stories were about his own hunts, others about his uncle's hunts or about Jim Corbett hunting man eaters. He had met the great hunter in the company of his uncle who was his close friend. He claimed that on one occasion he accompanied Jim Corbett and his uncle on a hunt for a man eater. That was his favorite story. He would point to the empty space on the wall and say, "That place is reserved for my tiger."

If someone enquired why he had not bagged a tiger, he would say, "When out alone I never saw a tiger. When hunting with friends, I always gave them the first shot."

There was another hunt about which he never mentioned anything. He would have removed it from his memory if he could, but its memory always haunted him. It was an incident that took place when, at the age of seventeen, his uncle had taken him on his first tiger hunt. A tiger had been spotted in a forest. A machan was erected on a tree in an open space in the forest and a goat was tied to a nearby tree as bait. John and his uncle mounted the machan late in the evening with the understanding that John would take the first shot. They would see any tiger approaching the goat in the bright moonlight night. After a few hours the tiger emerged from a clump of bushes. John became excited and fired a hasty shot. The tiger dashed back into the forest.

His uncle chided him gently, "You should have let it approach the goat and taken careful aim. We don't know whether you missed or wounded it. The rule of the jungle is that if you wound a tiger or a leopard you must track and kill it."

"Why is that so?" enquired John.

"The wound might cripple it. Then it won't be able to hunt its natural prey and be forced to hunt humans for food," replied his uncle."If this one is not wounded, there is a chance it might return. If it does not come we must search that spot in the morning for blood stains. If we find some, we must track it down and kill it. Tracking and killing a wounded tiger is very dangerous, but I have done it before."

The two remained on the machan the whole night, but the tiger did not return. Early in the morning, several men arrived from a nearby village led by the man who had provided the goat. The men had heard the shot and felt that the tiger had been killed. They came prepared to skin it and were disappointed when they did not see a dead tiger.

John and his uncle climbed down and they all carefully inspected the place for any signs of blood. They found only a large freshly killed rat- most probably accidentally crushed by the tiger. They spent the next four nights on the machan hoping for the tiger to return, but in vain. After that, the moon waned making the nights too dark for hunting.

Meanwhile their reputation went down in the eyes of the villagers. There was much talk in the village about two sahibs who had spent four nights to shoot a tiger but managed to shoot only a rat. The story spread and reached one of John's school mates and through him it spread in his school. Soon the entire school knew him by the title 'John the rat killer'.

Boys being boys, they made fun of him. Being a sensitive person he felt badly hurt by the teasing. It left a scar on his personality. To prove his hunting prowess he became a wanton killer of wild animals. He kept the best trophies for himself and gave away the rest to friends to further establish his reputation. Despite his best efforts he had not bagged a tiger so far. He had tried hunting them on foot by tracking them. Many times he had a fleeting glimpse of a tiger but no chance for an accurate shot. He had spent many days and nights on machans, but with no luck. He continued his quest to shoot a tiger with determination.

Today he felt that luck would favor him. A worker at his quarry had told him about a tiger sighted near his village. It had been seen several times, around noon, drinking water from a pond on the edge of the forest. The workman had erected the machan on which he sat waiting for the tiger.

He heard the sound of a large animal moving in the bushes near the pond. Soon a majestic deer, with huge antlers, emerged and walked gracefully to the pond. It took a quick look around and started drinking. It would make an excellent trophy but John was intent on a tiger. Suddenly the deer lifted its head and bounded away.

John was sure that it had caught the scent of a tiger. He was right. Soon the bushes parted and a tiger emerged. It stood on the edge of the forest and looked around carefully. Then turned its head towards the bushes and made a gentle whispering sound. Two small cubs emerged from the bushes. It was a tigress. It gently urged its cubs towards the pond and the cubs started drinking while the mother stood by protectively.

At first he thought of shooting the tigress and capturing the cubs to sell to some circus or zoo. He hesitated and watched the beautifully intimate scene with astonishment and joy. Never before had he seen dangerous wild creatures in such a peaceful setting. Now the mother also started drinking. They drank happily as if they were the gentlest of God's creatures. Then the tigress walked back and sat near the bushes while the two cubs fought playfully under her watchful eyes making gentle growling sounds. The mother cuffed them gently whenever they became too aggressive. John watched them with fascination for about ten minutes after which they went back into the forest.

John reflected over his past life. He wondered if it was right to take the lives of innocent animals. He returned home empty hand, but happy and at peace with himself. A sudden change had come over him. The idea of wanton killing revolted him.

He said to Alice, “My dear, from today I will kill only those animals which threaten human life. I promise to give up trophy hunting. I will also give away all of these trophies so that you may put up paintings and flowers in their place.”

She felt very happy and thanked him profusely and thanked God for this transformation.

****

Tales and Trivia from Academia IV

Coefficient of Restitution (CoR): It is a term used in the subject of Dynamics. If a ball falls on a horizontal surface then it rebounds to a lesser height. The ratio of the rebound height and the dropping height gives the value of the CoR of the material of the ball and the surface material. Its value is always less than one for all materials, because the ball bounces less each time it hits the surface.

A student asked, "Sir, are there any two materials whose CoR is greater than one."

The teacher replied "If two such materials existed, then the ball would bounce higher each successive time and finally bounce high enough to land on the moon."

This caused much laughter. A few days later that particular student was absent and so did not respond during attendance. The teacher repeated his name.

One student said, "Sir he has found two materials with CoR higher than one and has gone to visit the moon." This time even the teacher laughed along with all of the students.

Old PJs: A PJ is a poor joke. Some people detest PJs while others cherish old jokes and even enjoy old PJs. Here is a list of some old PJs: A Lecturer is defined as a person who talks while others sleep. A Professor is a person who professes to have great knowledge but might know very little. An Associate Professor is a person who associates with Professors. An Assistant Professor is a person who assists Professors. A Reader is a person who reads out his lecture notes in class.

Pendoo is the Physics teacher who loved to teach about the pendulum in great detail. Entropy is the nickname of the Physics Prof who lectured on the topic of Entropy for half of the semester, but no student understood anything about it.

Another Prof had specialized in Nuclear Physics, but most colleagues and students referred to his specialization as Unclear Physics because his knowledge of Physics was rather unclear. Mathematicians are known to be people who are willing to assume anything except responsibility. Maggoo was the student who spent most of his time mugging (meaning cramming and not street mugging). Later when he got married his wife was nicknamed as Mrs. Maggoo.

The Bus Trip: Once a bus trip was arranged for the final year Civil Engineering students to visit a construction site at Delhi. The bus capacity was fifty five seats and only thirty students gave their consent. The Prof in charge JMY invited other faculty members for the trip. Several accepted as they would get a free ride to Delhi and back and do some shopping or attend to some personal business at Delhi. The bus was scheduled to start from the department with the students at 5 am and pick up the faculty members at a few selected points. I was not aware of the trip, but later heard two versions- one from Professor DNY the person who missed the bus and the other from JMY. I have combined the two versions and narrated the story below.

On the day of the trip, I went to the tea club of the department and was surprised to see only one faculty member DNY present. He had missed the bus, and told me his version of the story even without my asking.

He was a middle aged bachelor who stayed alone. He said that the bus was due to leave at five in the morning. He did not have an alarm clock, so he decided to spend the whole night playing cards in the faculty club and then go to his quarters at 4 am and get ready to catch the bus. He would catch up on his sleep on the long journey to Delhi.

Unfortunately the staff club attendant closed the club at 12 midnight arguing that the normal closing time was 10-30 pm. No amount of coercion or bribe could make him wait any longer, as he had a four kilometer bicycle journey to his home. So DNY went to his PhD Scholar PRX's quarters and woke him up from deep sleep, and told him to wake him up at 4-30 am so that he would have half an hour to get ready and catch the bus.

The scholar set his alarm clock for 4-15 AM. When it rang he was extremely drowsy and went back to sleep. By the time he woke up again it was after 5am. He ran to wake DNY. In the meantime the bus had reached DNY's quarters. Prof JMY knocked on his door for several minutes before he woke up. Seeing that he was not ready he left saying that it will take DNY too long to get ready.

PRX reached there immediately afterwards. DNY asked him to run and stop the bus. The poor chap reached close to the bus and shouted to the driver to stop it, but to no avail. He ran fast and was just about to overtake it and would have stopped it. Unfortunately he had worn a lungi and just at that instant it came loose and started slipping down.

He had a difficult choice to make. First choice was to let the lungi fall down, be exposed stark naked and catch the bus. The second choice was to slow down and hold on to his lungi and let the bus go. Being an intelligent scholar he chose to hold on to his lungi and let the bus go. His decision caused annoyance to DNY, but was upheld by every sensible person.

Work in Workshop: A serious and pious student made a large poster with the words `Work is Worship.' He hung this over his study table in his hostel room, in order to inspire himself to study harder. Among his circle of best friends was a person, who was light-hearted, and had a fondness for satire. He promptly made a bigger poster with the words 'Work in Workshop` and hung it over his study table.

The Duster on the Fan: Some students play weird pranks. Once, a student placed a duster on one of the blades of the ceiling fan over the teacher's platform. Now this was a duster made of wood with a felt layer on one face. The Physics Prof came into the class, switched on the fan and started taking attendance. The fan blades spun faster and the duster fell on the floor making a loud noise, startling everyone.

The Prof remained calm and said, "It obeyed Newton's law of gravity."

His dignified response humbled the entire class and in particular the errant student who had committed the stupid act. After class he was admonished by his class mates. Later he went to the Prof's office and apologized.

The NCC Camp: At IIT, students had to choose between NCC and PT, both of which carried 100 marks each. A few students choose the former while the vast majority opted for the latter because it was far less rigorous. After the 1962 Indo-China war, the situation changed. NCC became compulsory for all. The worst part about NCC was the two weeks long camp. Firstly the camp food was far worse than the hostel food. Secondly it was held during the vacations. Most students would have gladly missed the camp for the joy of spending that time at their homes. Missing the camp meant a deduction of 25 marks. It was a very difficult choice and most students were in a dilemma.

The camp was during the summer vacations immediately following the exams. Some students decided to attend the camp, while some decided to forfeit the marks and go home. They did their packing accordingly. There were a few who wavered till the end. Among them were two close friends, SNX and ICY. The former was the 'Guru' while the latter was the 'Chela'.

Ten days before the camp SNX said, "Twenty-five marks are a lot, so let us go to camp."

ICY packed his stuff accordingly. The next day SNX changed his mind and said, "Let us skip the camp." ICY repacked his bags. SNX changed his mind half a dozen times. Each time ICY repacked his bags and the funny part was that SNX only packed his bags once according to his final decision. After this experience ICY decided to become his own 'Guru'.

****

Anuradha - The Beautiful

The two colleagues, Pranay and Krishna, were as unlike as chalk and cheese. The former was rather pushy, ill-mannered and prone to complain about everything. The latter was soft spoken and considerate. Pranay was married and had two kids while the latter was a bachelor. Both were executives in the same company at Hyderabad and of the same age. During tea breaks and lunch breaks they invariably sat together in the cafeteria. Pranay did most of the talking, which mostly consisted of complaints about everything and everyone under the sun. He was the most negative person Krishna had encountered. He would listen patiently, occasionally uttering a few words in agreement just to mollify Pranay, as he knew that it was no use contradicting him.

After months of listening to Pranay's complaints, he decided to do something about it in a tactful manner.

Sitting with him at lunchtime he said "Pranay let me tell you a true story about a girl who was the embodiment of grace, beauty and brains."

Pranay replied, "Ok, I will listen if it is interesting."

"It is really good," said Krishna, "and it provides an insight into human nature and it failings. Please do not interrupt otherwise I may lose the plot."

A girl named Anuradha was born and brought up in an educated, middle class family of Delhi. Her family and close friends called her Anu. She had a brother named Sirish and a sister named Anjana, both older than her. As the youngest child she was the most pampered. This made her headstrong and obstinate. Her brother and sister were good students, but she was far better. She always stood first in her class. She also took keen interest in music, painting, sports and debates and won numerous prizes. As Anu grew up she became prettier and more graceful by the day.

In her final year of school she decided to appear for the medical as well as engineering entrance tests. Her elder brother and sister had both chosen the engineering competitions and had qualified. Hence her family advised her to choose one and put in her undivided effort. She argued that she had excelled at studies and other activities simultaneously and so she could tackle both competitions together. As usual Anu's opinion prevailed. It came as a pleasant surprise when she secured such high ranks that she could choose any medical college or branch of engineering at any IIT.

The family urged her to choose engineering. In four years she would get her degree and also land a high paying job in a multinational company and get married soon. Medical studies would require double the time as she would have to complete MBBS followed by an internship and a post graduate specialization before she could get a good job or be a success in a private practice. Marriage would also be delayed.

They reasoned that, with her good looks they could get her married to an IAS officer or a high paid executive in a multinational and also it was not essential for her to work. She countered by saying that these were typical middle class views not suited for her generation. She also felt that medical studies were more challenging than engineering and a doctor could directly serve other human beings by curing their ailments and suffering.

She chose the MBBS program at AIIMS, the most prestigious medical institute in the country. As always her performance was brilliant. Time flew by and Sirish and Anjana were employed in good jobs and married before Anu could start her postgraduate studies. Most girls preferred gynecology but she preferred cardiology because an increasingly sedentary life style and high intake of fattening foods was causing a rapid increase in the number of heart patients in India. She wanted to join the fight against this major problem.

After completing her studies, she secured a good job in a cardiac hospital where she had the benefit of working with several renowned doctors. Her parents were keen to get her married. There was no dearth of proposals from highly qualified doctors, IAS officers and others. She did not want to marry a doctor, because then both husband and wife would be in highly demanding jobs and the home would be neglected. A man in a less demanding profession with flexible working hours would be preferable.

There were several such suitors including Govind who was their next door neighbor and a good friend and class mate of Sirish. Her family was strongly in his favor. He met her to plead his case, but she turned him down saying that she regarded him as an elder brother and so could not be romantically involved with him. She told her parents that marriage could wait till she established her reputation as a doctor. She would certainly get married when the time was right and would prefer to make her own choice.

People considered her to be the prettiest lady doctor in Delhi; some even argued that she was the prettiest in the country. Soon afterwards, Naresh arrived on the scene. He was a medical representative from a small town, lower middle class background with the good looks of a film star. This and his smooth talk and charm had won him many girl friends in the past. He soon found out that Dr. Anuradha wanted to marry a man who would take full charge of running the home. Posing as such a person, he used his charm and smooth talk to win her over. Her family and friends were shocked by her choice.

Her father said, "He is clearly unfit to be your husband. There is a big difference in status, education and income."

Anu replied, "He is a handsome, charming and caring person. He will be a supportive husband who will manage the home. A reputed pharmacy company hires only honest people. You have always opposed my choice of studies and career but I have been right. I am sure that I will be happy with him."

Naresh and Anu rented a flat near her hospital and occupied it after their marriage. They hired maids for the house work and Naresh took charge of all of the other mundane matters like purchasing, repairs and finances. He played the role of a loving and caring husband to perfection. Alas this happy state would not last long. She became pregnant and moved to her family home in the later stages and delivered a healthy baby boy. When the child was a month old, she shifted back to the flat.

Naresh's behavior had changed. He had stopped taking interest in household matters. When she complained about it, he replied sarcastically, "Anu dear, the honeymoon is over. Managing the house is a women's job. Don't expect me to do your job for the rest of my life."

She was too stunned to reply. He started returning home rather drunk and ignored her protests. On one occasion he said "For your sake I abstained from drinks, parties and women for almost a year. It was shear torture. Let me enjoy drinking and partying and I won't stop you from doing the same."

She screamed and slapped him. In return he beat her badly. Such fights became frequent and after one particularly severe beating she left for her parent's house with the child. Her father and Sirish were in favor of divorce but she, her mother and sister in law wanted to save the marriage. Sirish brought his friend Govind to advise her to opt for divorce.

Govind said, "Anu dear, your plight has made me very sad. I have been in love with you ever since I entered my teens. Please don't try to save this disastrous marriage. Get a divorce and I shall marry you and treat your son as my own."

Again she turned him down saying that she had always been successful at anything she attempted and was determined to make her marriage succeed. Naresh's parents were informed and they came to Delhi. They said that Naresh must have picked up bad habits after getting a job in Delhi. They took Anu's side and blamed their son for his disgraceful behavior. Under pressure from both families, Naresh agreed to enter a rehabilitation center for his drinks and drugs addiction.

On his discharge after over two months he was advised to report once a week for follow up assessment and medication. Anu wanted to shift back to their flat with the child, but her family advised against taking the child. Sirish's wife, who was childless, refused to allow her to take the boy. Naresh's mother came to live with the couple to ensure that he did not go back to his drunken ways. As agreed by the two families, Sirish engaged a detective agency to keep a watch on Naresh.

For a few months the situation was normal but then Naresh's mother had to leave. Soon after, he returned to his drinks and drugs. The detective agency gave details of his affairs with two women. Anu thought that the best way to break up these affairs would be to catch him red handed. One morning she followed him discreetly and sure enough he went to the house of one of the women reported by the agency. It was on a small plot in a quiet area and had three floors. Seeing Naresh enter the ground floor, she waited for a few minutes and then entered the gate and peeped through the front window. Naresh was seated on a sofa with one arm around a woman and the other hand holding a glass. A whisky bottle stood on the low table in front.

She stood still frozen with disgust. Then she rang the bell. The woman opened the door and stood with an enquiring look in her eyes. Seeing her to be an older woman, Anu's feeling of disgust increased. Sidestepping the woman she went up to Naresh and said, "You drunkard, get up and come home immediately to sober down."

The woman spoke. "How dare you enter my house and shout at my boy friend!"

Anu replied, "He happens to be my husband".

The woman retorted, "He comes to me because you are a rotten wife."

Anu answered back, "You are old enough to be his mother."

The woman's face turned red with anger and she rushed to the kitchen and came back brandishing a sharp pointed knife. She advanced on Anu and shouted, "You bitch! One small prick and you will go running with your tail between your legs."

Anu retreated but was stopped by a chair. The knife came close to her stomach. In panic she grabbed the woman's wrist. The two struggled and fell. Getting up Anu saw the woman lying on the ground with the knife embedded in her chest. She was struggling to breathe. Anu pulled out the knife to try to save her. Now Naresh stood up and lurched drunkenly towards her saying, "I won't let you escape."

She pointed the knife towards him to keep him at bay, but he tripped on the carpet and fell towards her. The knife pierced his chest and slipped from her hand and the fall pushed it deep into his heart. She bent down to pull it out but he was dead. By now the woman had also stopped breathing. Anu fainted and fell on a sofa and lay there for several minutes.

When she revived, she saw the gruesome scene, with the bodies and the spilled blood. She needed to get out from the place quickly. She went out and walked on the street for a while to calm her nerves. She went into a restaurant and ordered a cup of coffee. Taking out her note pad, she wrote a letter to her father about the killings and her decision to end her life, as she could not bear to face trial and imprisonment. It would also bring disgrace to her family and ruin her child's life. She wanted Sirish and his wife to adopt her son, and never let him know about his real parents to save him from trauma. She deeply regretted her decisions to turn down Govind and marry Naresh. She requested Sirish to persuade Govind to get married soon otherwise her soul would not rest in peace. After giving the letter to a courier she walked back to the house of death and slit her wrists with the blood stained knife.

Pranay, who had been listening attentively, hesitated for a moment and commented, "My heart bleeds for Anu. If Naresh had truly reformed, the story would have a happy ending, but that is life. Anu paid a very heavy price for her one mistake. Maybe her academic successes made her arrogant and she thought herself to be a better judge of human nature than her parents."

"That may be so, but it is very difficult to judge a person's real nature. I do not blame her," countered Krishna.

"I bet the guy named Govind is you and you have given fake names to Anuradha and her relations to protect their privacy," said Pranay.

"Yes, your guess is correct. I am that unfortunate person," replied Krishna. "My mistake was that I accepted her first refusal. I should have persisted till she gave in. Then she would be happily married to me. Fortunately she did not die."

"How is that possible?" enquired Pranay, "You mentioned that she had slashed her wrists."

"Luckily a courier came to the house and looked into the window and raised an alarm. She was rushed to the hospital and her life was saved," replied Krishna. "She was tried in court and given a lenient sentence of three years, because both of the killings were accidental. She will be released in a few months."

"I suppose you have not married because you are waiting for her," said Pranay.

"You guessed right again. This time I will not take no for an answer," replied Krishna. "I have her letter in which she urged that I should get married. I will use that to persuade her to accept my proposal."

"I am sure you will succeed," was Pranay's response.

Krishna was happy that at last Pranay had said something positive.

****

The Travelling Professor

Everyone referred to Prof CDY as the travelling Prof. His study of flora, fauna and an interest in geology made it necessary for him to visit different parts of the country. He had many varied experiences during his travels- some peculiar, some funny and others unpleasant. This is a brief narration of the more notable ones.

Once he travelled to a small town in a far off state by train. There he purchased a first class ticket for a bus which also offered second and third class tickets. On boarding the bus he was dismayed to see that all tickets holders could sit wherever they chose to do so.

He asked the conductor, "What is the use of paying extra for the first class tickets, if I have to sit with everyone else?"

The latter replied, "Sir, you will find out soon." Within minutes the bus was full and the conductor announced, "First class passengers please remain seated. Second and third class passengers get down. Third class passengers push the bus to make it start." Every time the bus halted the same routine was repeated. Thus Prof CDY realized the benefit of the first class ticket.

Another time he took a group of PG students to a National Wildlife Park to study the flora and fauna. A mother elephant and its calf were wandering around. CDY did not see them and started collecting some plants specimens which were between the two. The mother elephant charged towards him. He ran, tripped and fell into a dry, narrow water course. The elephant tried to crush him with its head but the water course was too narrow. The students heard his screams and they shouted and threw stones at the elephant which left him and rushed towards its calf. His life was saved, though he suffered a few bruises and a fracture of the arm.

Our intrepid traveler did not allow the encounter with the elephant to deter him. His next visit was to the rural area of another state. Walking around in search of specimens he chanced upon a rural school. Being tired and thirsty he entered the school and introduced himself. The Principal and the Vice Principal invited him to their office as an honored guest and asked him if he would have a cup of tea. He gave his consent happily. The Principal made a peculiar three finger gesture to the peon who brought a cup of tea, with a plate under the cup and another one covering it.

This was placed in front of CDY. He removed the top plate and was disappointed to see the extremely small size of the cup. When he started drinking, the Principal and the Vice Principal gave him a look of surprise but said nothing. That evening at dinner time he spoke with his hotel manager and told him about the peculiar experience and the three finger gesture for ordering tea.

The manager replied, "Sir, that gesture is for one cup of tea to be shared between three persons. That is why there was an extra plate covering the cup. It was placed in front of you because you were the guest. Any local guest would have poured some tea into each of the two plates for the other two and drank the rest from the cup." In this way CDY learned that he had unwittingly violated the local traditions of hospitality.

His next visit took him to another far off state. After an overnight train journey he boarded a bus for a small town. He placed his suitcase and holdall on the roof of the bus and sat on a window seat. Soon the bus filled up but it did not start. He could hear some sounds on the roof. He thought it was luggage being loaded. Suddenly two objects fell from the roof with a load impact on the ground. One of them narrowly missed his elbow, which was protruding from the window. It surprised him to see that the objects were his suitcase and holdall. He got down angrily and saw a large group of men sitting on the roof. He enquired who had thrown his luggage.

A man shouted back, "The roof is for sitting not for luggage." CDY, though shocked, asked boldly, "Then where should I put my luggage."

The answer from the roof was, "Put it on your head." By now the passenger next to him had climbed down. He helped CDY take his luggage inside and adjust it under the seats. During the journey they talked with each other. He was a local man, familiar with the region and helpful. At journey's end he took CDY to a comfortable hotel and told the manager to treat CDY like a VIP guest and give him a heavy discount. Then he and CDY had lunch. The manger refused to accept payment for the lunch.During the stay CDY did get VIP treatment. The manager and the staff treated him like a visiting dignitary.

When he asked the manager about his travelling companion, the latter looked surprised and said, "You came with him so I thought he is your friend. He is the biggest Don in this area. His gang loots the trucks in this region. Almost all truckers pay him protection money."

Hearing this, CDY was stunned. This Don had treated him far better than those uncouth men who had thrown down his luggage and insulted him. Then he concluded that a criminal can also behave like a gentleman.

****

The Ghost Couple

The day and time were most suitable for ghosts. Even the weather and place were to the liking of any ghost. Vijay was on an extended visit to his cousin Arun, who lived in a three hundred year old haveli with his parents Mr. and Mrs. Kanodia and an elder brother, Suresh. Vijay was fascinated by the old haveli, its architecture, its old style doors, windows, antique furniture, and the colorful wall paintings. This was his first visit and he found it to be most interesting and enjoyable.

Vijay and Arun studied in the same boarding school and were in the same class. They had known each other since the day they were admitted to the school. They were close friends as well as first cousins. Arun had given vivid descriptions of the haveli to Vijay. They had long wanted that Vijay should spend the summer vacations at the haveli. Finally after much begging and pleading Vijay's parents had agreed. A month had passed too quickly for both boys. Now the rainy season had started.

It was evening time on that day, the time when ghosts stir in their grave and creep out to scare humans. It was raining heavily with frequent flashes of lightning followed by deafening sounds of thunder. Arun's brother was in his room busy pursuing his hobby of painting. His parents had gone to see a play and planned to return late in the evening. When they left the sky was clear. After a while, dark clouds had appeared suddenly.

Arun said to Vijay, "Let us play a trick on mother and father."

"What kind of trick?"

"Let us dress up as ghosts and scare them."

Vijay hesitated and said, "That won't be nice. What will they think of me?"

"Oh, come on! Don't be so formal. You are a part of the family. After all, your mother is dad's sister. Can't you, for once, do as I say without a fuss?"

"Ok, if you say so!"

Vijay had heard that the house was haunted. Well any house which is three hundred years old is bound to be haunted- specially this haveli. When darkness set in, it looked frightening– exactly like haunted houses in movies. Unknown to most people the house did have ghosts of old family ancestors. One was a male, who had been murdered in the prime of his youth and had become a ghost. He had been an introvert and timid person, who had been fond of good food. He did not use his ghostly powers to scare the inhabitants of the house. After all they were his descendants. As a ghost he avoided being seen and rarely came out, except when he got the scent of good food. Then he would come to the kitchen to inhale the aroma, being careful not to arouse suspicion. Even so, the cook or the maid saw him sometimes. These sightings were dismissed by Arun's parents as figments of their imagination.

There was a second ghost also, a female who had never been seen. She was the wife of the murdered man and had lived for many years in the home after his death, taking good care of their children. After death she had remained there as a ghost in the company of her husband. She spent her time praying for the salvation of her husband and her own so that they could go to heaven.

Hurriedly the two boys made preparations. Arun said, "I will get some old, white sheets from the store room and some black ink."

"And scissors also," added Vijay.

'What for, dimwit?'

'To cut your hair short, you fool.'

"Why not cut your own hair and turn you into a bald ghost."

Vijay said, "Couldn't you guess that we need the scissors to cut eye holes in the sheets."

"You should have said that."

"I thought you had brains enough to understand."

"Oh come on, let us not argue. They might be arriving soon."

Vijay cut the eye holes and Arun used the black ink to draw skulls and cross bones. They covered themselves with the sheets. So that the eye holes matched with their eyes and the skull and cross bones appeared on the chest. They looked at each other and were satisfied that they looked like ghosts. Then they switched of the main lights of the hall and let some light come in from the side room. In the dim light they looked even scarier.

The plan was to leave the front door slightly ajar for the parents to enter. Vijay would stand in the center of the hall and make a moaning sound to scare Arun's parents. Arun would stand inside a cupboard and come out suddenly making load hissing sounds. This would surely scare his parents enough to send them running out of the house. Afterwards they would take off their sheets and laugh loudly. The parents would join in their laughter feeling relieved that there were no ghosts. This is what they imagined, but the situation turned out to be different.

Suddenly, Vijay sensed the presence of a third person. He looked towards the side room door. He saw a figure similar to him and Arun, but considerably taller. He thought it must be Suresh come to join in the fun, but it was the ghost. He had overheard their plan and was annoyed that two mischievous boys were planning a trick. He had come to teach them a lesson which they would not forget soon.

Vijay pointed towards the shadowy figure and said, "Arun your brother has come to help us."

Arun looked in that direction and saw nothing. He said, "Now that you are playing the role of a ghost, you have started seeing them."

Vijay had really seen the ghost, but he had vanished immediately. In his days children were brought up to be obedient and respectful towards their elders. He was appalled that some of his descendants should take such liberties with their elders. He spoke about it with his wife. She agreed with him that the children should be taught a lesson.

Together they had made a plan to discipline the children. Now they put it into action. They assumed the shapes of Arun's parents and entered the hall though the door left ajar. Vijay made a moaning sound and Arun came out of the cupboard making hissing sounds. The children heard them scream in an unearthly manner. This chilled their blood. Then they saw them dash out of the front door and heard loud sounds of large bodies falling on the floor one after the other.

The two boys rushed out and saw Mr. and Mrs. Kanodia lying motionless on the verandah floor. They were not sure if the couple were play acting, or had fainted due to fright. When Arun's parents did not stir for almost half a minute, the two bent down and felt their wrists. They felt cold, clammy and lifeless. Now it was their turn to emit unearthly screams. They ran back into the hall in fright.

As soon as they recovered their senses Vijay said, "You get your elder brother, I will look for the driver. We must take them to the hospital immediately."

Arun rushed to fetch his brother, but he was nowhere to be seen. The servant and the maid were also missing. Vijay went to the garage to look for the driver and the car but they were not there. He called out loudly, but got no response. He could not find anyone in the servant quarter also. Meanwhile Arun tried the phone, but found it dead. The two boys returned to the verandah at the same time. They saw the two bodies as they had left them. They felt utterly helpless and started sobbing loudly.

After a minute or so a car drove up to the gate. The driver got down to open the gate and drove the car to the verandah. Mr. and Mrs. Kanodia stepped out and were surprised to see the two boys sitting on the floor and sobbing loudly. Arun and Vijay looked back and were shocked to see them standing. They got an even bigger shock when they saw that the bodies had vanished.

Mrs. Kanodia was concerned and asked, "Why are you two weeping? Has Suresh beaten you?"

By now Vijay had got his composure back. He replied, "Nothing like that. We were simply rehearsing for our school drama." This satisfied the parents who said nothing more.

Later Arun said to Vijay, "You are a quick thinker. You covered up everything so well. Now I am quite sure that we have ghosts in our house. I won't tell anything to mom and dad because they won't believe what happened."

That night both Vijay and Arun had identical dreams. They saw two ghosts. The male said, "We are the ghosts of two of your long dead ancestors. We are forced to remain in this house forever. We overheard your plan to trick and scare your elders. We wanted to teach you a lesson so that you will learn to respect them. If you do not behave in the future, we will give you an even severer lesson. We can also go to your school or any other place to scare you."

Then the female spoke. Her voice was gentle and motherly. She said, "I was also upset that you do not respect your elders. I am unhappy that we scared you more we than intended. Please forgive us. What we did was necessary to teach you a lesson. Let this occurrence be a secret between us. We don't want to give this haveli the reputation of a haunted house."

Both boys gave identical replies, "We have learned the lesson and will keep your secret. We will pray for your release so that you can go to heaven."

****

The Summer Training

At the end of the pre-final year, engineering students used to undergo a one month long practical training during the summer vacation. Today this is called internship. A fellow student and I were assigned to a construction project in Delhi. The CPWD was supervising the construction of two large office buildings. We reported to the Assistant Engineer (AE), an elderly person, who was in-charge at the site. There were several Junior Engineers (JEs) under him.

Every few days an Executive Engineer used to visit the site and review the progress and issue instructions. During his visits the AE and the JEs treated him with great respect and fear. Occasionally the Superintending Engineer used to come with the EE. On those occasions the AE and the JEs used to be quite tense. Above all of them there was a Chief Engineer. Fortunately his visit did not materialize during our brief period there.

The AE had assigned us to one of the JEs who showed us the drawings and explained the construction details. One of the buildings had a drum shaped plan; the other one had a y-shaped plan. The latter was in the finishing stage while the former was under construction. The work was a new experience for us and we were keen to learn. We carefully observed the setting up of the formwork, shuttering and staging, cutting, bending and placing of reinforcement and the mixing and pouring of concrete.

One day the AE said, “Tomorrow you will see something most important and interesting. You will learn a lot.”

They had decided to connect the water supply line for one building. The pipe line had been laid almost up to the main water supply line which ran parallel to the main road in front of the building. Before noon a pit was dug to expose a small segment of the main line.

It was decided to make the connection during the afternoon. A T-pipe was used to make the junction. Its leg was of the size of the building supply line which was of a small diameter while and the head pipe was of a large diameter to match the main supply line. A man entered the pit. He had a huge hammer with which to shatter one segment of the main line. The head of the T-pipe would then be joined with the main pipe and the leg with the building pipe.

Unfortunately, they had forgotten to turn off the water supply in the main line. As soon as the man hit the main line, it shattered and water gushed out and filled the pit and overflowed on the main road. The AE was very angry and shouted at the JEs. Some of them along with the mistri and some laborers rushed to the nearby water supply office to close the valve. They returned after a few minutes and laborers started digging soil to make an embankment around the pit and then started baling the water out using buckets and pans. Still the water could not be removed completely because more water was coming out. At first it was thought that it was the residual water flowing out, but the flow did not stop even after a long time.

Then the AE sent the contractor and some men to check if the valve had been closed completely. After a while the contractor reported that he had now personally closed the valve completely. Soon the flow of water stopped and the pit was emptied after frantic baling.

The T-pipe was lowered into the pit and connected to join the house pipe and main pipe ends with the help of couplers. A fire was lit and some lead was melted and poured into the three joints to seal them properly. It was almost 8 pm and we were keen to return home, but the AE asked us to accompany him to his first floor office because a very important task had to be completed. He made a phone call to the Chief Engineer's residence. A servant responded. The AE said, "I am the AE from the site and have an urgent message for Chief Sahib."

As soon as the Chief was on the line, the AE stood up at attention and said, "Sir, I have completed the water supply connection to the y-shaped building. Tomorrow we will check all internal pipes and taps for leakage."

This important task completed, he asked us, "Did you learn much today?"

We nodded our heads in agreement. Then he said, "You have learned two very important lessons today. Number one is how to make the water supply connection. Number two how to speak with a Chief Engineer with proper respect."

At that time I was staying with my uncle in New Delhi. By the time I reached home it was almost 9 PM and both my aunt and uncle were extremely worried. My friend had his home in Old Delhi and he reached home much later than 9 PM and his parents were even more worried. If the valve had been closed before starting, the work would have been completed by 4 pm latest.

During our stay we had gained valuable practical knowledge. We also learned about the cult of bossism in which the Chief Engineer was like a demi god. The biggest lesson we learned that day was that greater care should be taken to avoid such silly mistakes.

****

About the Author

Kiran Kumar Singh

The author, Dr. Kiran Kumar Singh, was born in Agra in 1945. He was married to Reba Rautela, a highly skilled artist who passed away in 2017. He studied at IIT, Kharagpur and in USA and retired from IIT, Roorkee as a Professor. He received the Lifetime Achievement Award of the Indian Concrete Institute at Roorkee in February 2024. Reading, writing, tennis and philately are his main interests.

He has authored four books-two science fiction adventure novels, a biography of a noted educationist and a book of true inspiring short stories based on the lives of people who struggled to rise from obscurity. He has made online presentations of his Science Fiction novels at conferences organized by the Indian Association of Science Fiction Studies and has published a review paper on a collection of twelve science fiction short stories.

Milton Keynes UK
Ingram Content Group UK Ltd.
UKHW030658151124
451186UK00005B/56

9 789367 958728